"What are the chances she'll want to talk to me?" Zach asked.

"One hundred percent." Fran was sure about that.

That stopped him again. "You think she'll have questions?"

"I know she has questions. She's had them about her uncle Zach for a long time. Being told you're her biological father raised more. And now that you've shown up, there will be even more questions."

"What kind of questions?"

"You'll see." And she smiled.

"That's not reassuring, Fran."

Her smile deepened. "It wasn't meant to be."

Dear Reader,

June, the ideal month for weddings, is the perfect time to celebrate true love. And we are doing it in style here at Silhouette Special Edition as we celebrate the conclusion of several wonderful series. With *For the Love of Pete*, Sherryl Woods happily marries off the last of her ROSE COTTAGE SISTERS. It's Jo's turn this time—and she'd thought she'd gotten Pete Catlett out of her system for good. But at her childhood haven, anything can happen! Next, MONTANA MAVERICKS: GOLD RUSH GROOMS concludes with Cheryl St.John's *Million-Dollar Makeover*. We finally learn the identity of the true heir to the Queen of Hearts Mine—and no one is more shocked than the owner herself, the plain-Jane town... dog walker. When she finds herself in need of financial advice, she consults devastatingly handsome Riley Douglas—but she soon finds his influence exceeds the business sphere....

And speaking of conclusions, Judy Duarte finishes off her BAYSIDE BACHELORS miniseries with *The Matchmakers' Daddy*, in which a wrongly imprisoned ex-con finds all kinds of second chances with a beautiful single mother and her adorable little girls. Next up in GOING HOME, Christine Flynn's heartwarming miniseries, is *The Sugar House*, in which a man who comes home to right a wrong finds himself falling for the woman who's always seen him as her adversary. Patricia McLinn's next book in her SOMETHING OLD, SOMETHING NEW... miniseries, *Baby Blues and Wedding Bells*, tells the story of a man who suddenly learns that his niece is really...his daughter. And in *The Secrets Between Them* by Nikki Benjamin, a divorced woman who's falling hard for her gardener learns that he is in reality an investigator hired by her ex-father-in-law to try to prove her an unfit mother.

So enjoy all those beautiful weddings, and be sure to come back next month! Here's hoping you catch the bouquet....

Gail Chasan
Senior Editor

Please address questions and book requests to:
Silhouette Reader Service
U.S.: 3010 Walden Ave., P.O. Box 1325, Buffalo, NY 14269
Canadian: P.O. Box 609, Fort Erie, Ont. L2A 5X3

BABY BLUES AND WEDDING BELLS

PATRICIA McLINN

SPECIAL EDITION

Published by Silhouette Books

America's Publisher of Contemporary Romance

With much appreciation to:

Michael T. Stieber of the Morton Arboretum in Lislé, Illinois,
and Wendy Steers of Heritage Hill in Green Bay, Wisconsin.

The staff at McLean (Virginia) Animal Hospital and Kathy Neil
of Rose Haven Collies.

And, especially, medical specialist Ron Sacra and
Lieutenant Mark D. Stone of Virginia Task Force One, the International
Urban Search and Rescue team of Fairfax County, Virginia.

 SILHOUETTE BOOKS

ISBN 0-373-24691-9

BABY BLUES AND WEDDING BELLS

Copyright © 2005 by Patricia McLaughlin

Visit Silhouette Books at www.eHarlequin.com

Printed in U.S.A.

Books by Patricia McLinn

PATRICIA McLINN

finds great satisfaction in transferring the characters crowded in her head onto paper to be enjoyed by readers. "Writing," she says, "is the hardest work I'd never give up." Writing has brought her new experiences, places and friends—especially friends. After degrees from Northwestern University, newspaper jobs have taken her from Illinois to North Carolina to Washington, D.C. Patricia now lives in Virginia, in a house that grows piles of paper, books and dog hair at an alarming rate. The paper and books are her own fault, but the dog hair comes from a charismatic collie, who helps put things in perspective when neighborhood kids refer to Patricia as "the lady who lives in Riley's house." She would love to hear from readers at P.O. Box 7052, Arlington, VA 22207 or you can check out her Web site at www.PatriciaMcLinn.com.

Chapter One

Nothing had changed in the past eight and half years. Not here on Lakeview Street.

The house rose like a secular cathedral from the highest point in town, looking down on Lake Tobias. The grounds were precise and polished...and nowhere near as inviting as the Daltons' homey yard next door.

No, nothing had changed at Corbett House.

Zach Corbett found that oddly reassuring.

Reassuring because so much else had changed. What he'd seen of the rest of Tobias, Wisconsin, had included fresh buildings, unfamiliar roads and new businesses. And he'd changed, that was for damn sure.

Odd, because Corbett House—the upright, pristine architectural embodiment of the Corbett Ideal as expounded and practiced by his mother, Lana Corbett—represented the reason he'd left. So how could he feel reassured that it hadn't changed?

Maybe because it meant this might actually be a routine run, like Doc had talked about.

Yeah, right.

Standing in front of the Daltons' home, he stared across the wide lawns to the house where he'd grown up. No, that wasn't true. He hadn't grown up in that house at all. He'd stayed a child there. He hadn't grown up until he'd left.

So why did he even need to be here? He had a life, far from Tobias in more ways than geography. He didn't have anything to prove. Not anymore. If it hadn't been for the old man Miguel—

"Go ahead. Someone will answer if you knock."

Zach remained still, not jolting or overreacting at the unexpectedness of the calm voice. Not reacting at all, except to listen more closely. To try to pinpoint where the voice had come from. The faintest sound could make all the difference. That had been drummed into him by training and experience.

But it took little of either—training or experience—to determine the source of this sound. All he had to do was move his eyes.

She must have been there all along. A compact female figure in tan and green, who blended in with a corner bed of bushes and flowers where the Daltons' property met the Corbetts' and the front sidewalk. She was crouched down, a trowel in one gloved hand and a clump of weeds in the other.

He'd have spotted her long before she spoke if she'd moved. She must have seen him coming and chosen not to give herself away. Because she hadn't recognized him? Or because she had?

"Or is that the problem—that someone will answer if you knock?"

As she spoke the second time, she straightened. The leaves

of the biggest bush, losing their full summer green, rested on the crown of her shining hair.

Fran Dalton hadn't grown very tall, he decided as he surveyed the figure beneath the green shirt and tan jeans, but she had grown up. When he'd left she'd been the quiet, plump girl who'd lived next door all his life. She was no longer plump, though nicely rounded where a woman should be. Her wavy hair, a lighter brown where a summer's worth of sun had reached it, was drawn back in a short, loose braid.

One thing hadn't changed—the way she looked at him. Neither glaring, as most of Tobias's adults used to, nor batting her eyelashes at him and blushing—or *not* blushing, but instead blatantly inviting—like his female contemporaries had. Fran Dalton still looked him straight in the eyes with no bull.

She was a year younger than him, two years younger than their older brothers, who'd been best friends.

Steve. That was one good thing about getting this over with. Once Zach had faced down Lana, he'd go looking for his older brother.

Zach grinned, a warmth spreading through his chest. "Hi, Franny."

"Hello, Zachary."

His grin widened. "Still don't like that nickname, huh?"

"Still don't like your given name?"

He dropped the grin, and the teasing. "How are you, Fran?" He really wanted to know.

"I'm very well, thank you. You look …" Her gaze skimmed his face, no doubt seeing the hardening of the years and life, then came back to his eyes and stayed there a long moment before she completed her assessment. "Good."

"So do you. Real good." That cut no ice with her, he saw—

either she didn't believe it or she wasn't interested. "You back here visiting your family? How are they?"

She shook her head. "I live here. Dad got sick, and I moved back. I never left after he died." She continued quickly, "So the family's just me and Rob."

"I'm sorry to hear about your dad. He was a good man."

"Yes, he was."

"But no nieces and nephews? I thought Rob was going to marry that girl from college. Jan? Janet?"

Rob was her older brother, Steve's best friend. Asking about her family, not his—oh, yeah, he was definitely procrastinating. But he was the only one who knew, so what could a few more minutes hurt.

"Janice. They did get married. No kids and they divorced. But he's found the right one now."

Her mouth lifted and her eyes glinted—there was more to her brother's story than those bare facts, and it pleased her. He'd like to find out more about that later…if there was a later.

"How's…" He tipped his head toward Corbett House.

Amusement fled from her expression. "You'll have to find that out for yourself, Zach. They've been so worried about you. Steve still puts ads—"

"Steve's in Tobias?"

Damn, he'd hoped his older brother had escaped, too. But Steve always had thought he could be his own kind of Corbett, even in Tobias. He'd wanted a life outside Lana's social and political ambitions, starting with going against her wishes by planning to marry his hometown sweetheart. Zach had left months before the wedding date; not standing up as his brother's best man when—if—he married Annette Trevetti was his one regret.

"Yes, he and Annette live—"

"He and Annette?" So, Steve *had* withstood Lana's disapproval of what she considered a misalliance with a girl from the wrong side of town. "I didn't know if he could pull it off, but he married her, huh? Good for him."

"Yes, they're married. Now. But…" A frown pulled the smooth arch of her brows into a straight line and worry swirled in her eyes.

"What is it, Fran? Steve's not— Is he okay?"

"I can't… You can't expect me—anyone—to fill in the years between you and your family, Zach." She shook her head, as if the firm determination of her words hadn't been enough. "You have to do this yourself."

And that brought them back to what she'd first said to him: *Someone will answer if you knock…. Or is that the problem?*

Maybe he wasn't the only one who'd known he was procrastinating.

There the house sat, as sure of itself as always. The immaculate landscaping, the broad stairs, the wide porch, and inside, room after frozen room. All designed to impress. Pure Corbett, right to the floor plan.

He could walk away now and Fran could tell them he was okay. Steve would believe Fran. Zach could go back. Back to where he belonged, back to where he'd made a life. And this would be enough to let him pick up that life again. Surely it would be enough.

He would write a letter. That would be better, easier, for everyone. That's what he should have done in the first place, instead of this—what? Pilgrimage? Penance?

He'd done pretty well for himself far from Tobias. Found a good life. Just because Taz thought he needed a break didn't mean he had to spend the time here. He could go back, take

Verdi up on the offer of his place at the beach. Or help Waco build that cabin in the mountains.

He had other places to go. Places he knew he'd be welcomed. As he was, not as anyone wanted him to be.

Yeah, he could turn around and leave. Again.

The old man. His hold on Zach's arm so strong. His eyes bright and intense against the gray of his face.

And Doc's voice. *You need to deal with it, Zach. Now, before it gets worse.*

"You've come this far, Zach," Fran said. "And you must have come for a reason."

God, you'd think she and Doc were in cahoots.

His neck felt stiff as he turned away from Corbett House and looked at her. He manufactured a grin. "Just to let them know I'm alive."

"That's a start," she said evenly. "So you better go do it."

"Yeah."

He'd known this wasn't going to be fun. But the reality had him wishing he could stand here on the sidewalk and talk to Fran awhile longer. Ask what she'd been doing with her life, listen to her smooth voice, maybe even tell her some of what he'd done. Would Fran believe he wasn't the kid he'd been?

Not that it mattered. He hadn't come back for redemption. He'd come back because an old man's grip hadn't let go even after three months.

The past will not stop speaking to you....

He cleared his throat. "I doubt I'll be hanging around after…later, so I'll say goodbye now. It's good seeing you, Fran."

He reached toward her. He'd intended to cup her shoulder, a gesture of longtime neighbors, old friends. Instead, his hand traveled toward her cheek, poised to brush his knuckles slowly down the soft, cream slant.

He dropped his hand to his side without making contact. That was something else he'd learned—better to make no move rather than the wrong move. And touching Fran like that... Bad move, definitely a bad move.

A faint voice deep inside asked why it would be such a bad move, but he ignored it.

"It's been good seeing you, too, Zach." Fran regarded him with serious attention, as if reading his history in his face.

"Take care of yourself." A platitude, yet something about it ruffled the calm in her eyes.

"I do," she said.

And then she was looking at him again, expecting him to continue his journey to Corbett House, giving no quarter. He pivoted away from her. That was harder to do than he'd expected.

But in these past years, he'd learned to push on when so much inside him screamed to get out, to get away. He'd done a hell of a lot harder things than advance a few yards along the public sidewalk and turn left up the walk that paralleled Corbett House's curved drive.

Hell of a lot harder.

Halfway up the steps to the house, he paused and looked back.

Fran wasn't there. She wasn't anywhere in sight.

She'd meant it when she'd said it was up to him. He could turn and walk away and there would be no one to disapprove or applaud. No one but him.

He swore under his breath, then climbed the remaining steps to face the oversize dark wooden door that stood out like the entrance to a cave against the white clapboards at either side.

As a kid, he'd rarely used the front door. That had been re-served for important people. But he'd gone out the front door when he'd left more than eight years ago and he'd be damned if he would return any other way.

Ignoring the knocker, he drummed his knuckles against the wood, and waited.

Instead of thinking about what would happen next, his mind slid to the past few minutes.

Fran hadn't asked where he'd been, what he'd done. Prob-ably didn't care. Most people in this town thought life out-side of Tobias was a rumor. She'd come back and settled right in again, so she must have caught the disease, too. The To-bias Syndrome.

The thought twisted his mouth as the door opened wide.

Fran allowed herself only a few seconds of watching Zach before she hurried inside.

Those seconds had been long enough to confirm that she truly had recognized his walk when she'd first seen a man coming up Lakeview Street.

Hunched down under a yellow lilac to dig out the clover trying to take over, she'd sensed someone approaching. At first, with the afternoon light behind him, she'd seen only a male outline and the motion of his walk. Instantly, she'd known it was Zach Corbett.

Which made absolutely no sense, because what had been most recognizable about his walk was the slouching swagger. Girls in her class had gushed over it. She'd thought the whole thing rather silly. Couldn't they see he was pretending to be something he wasn't?

And now that slouching swagger was gone. Yet she'd recognized Zach by his walk. After eight and a half years, for heaven's sake.

She'd held perfectly still when he'd stopped a yard and a half from her and stared at his family home. She might have stayed hidden if she'd had a good view of his face. But curiosity and the sense that he was about to turn around and leave prompted her to make her presence known.

His eyes were still that sparkling blue that had often startled her. But now they lacked the burning anger that had been another of Zach Corbett's hallmarks.

She shook her head at herself. She didn't have time for this.

Even if Zach didn't reach the front door of Corbett House, Steve and Annette needed to know he had come back. Needed to know he was alive. Not only to clear the worry and pain she knew Steve, especially, had carried all these years since Zach had left, but for Nell's sake.

Oh, God—*Nell.*

Would Zach's appearance make it easier or harder for Steve and Annette's young daughter in the long run? No matter what, it made things infinitely more complicated for both Nell and her parents.

Fran grabbed the phone. She tried Steve and Annette Corbett's house first. She got their machine. This was not news Fran was going to leave in a message.

Steve's cell phone didn't go through. Annette's went directly to her messaging service. Next Fran tried Steve's Town Hall office. Steve's assistant said he was at Bliss House, checking a detail on the renovation of the nineteenth-century mansion into a crafts center. If he called in, she'd be sure to have him phone Fran.

Fran looked at the clock on the stove. Nell should be home from school by now. But maybe she'd gone to Bliss House to meet Steve or to visit Miss Trudi, who served as Nell's guide in her diverse interests. Miss Trudi, a retired art teacher, had donated Bliss House to the town when she could no longer keep up the crumbling seventeen-room structure. In exchange, snug, modern quarters had been built for her on the property.

But on the chance Nell had gone home to tend to her dog, Pansy, Fran went out the back door and through the screened porch with no more than a wave in response to the hello yip from Chester and her pups there, then started across the deep backyard. Like the yards of the other four houses in this over-size block, hers ran from Lakeview Street in the front to Kelly Street in back. Steve and Annette's house faced her backyard from the opposite side of Kelly Street.

They were her neighbors, they were fellow members on the committee renovating Bliss House, and they were her friends.

She knocked and called out. Pansy barked from inside. "Sorry, girl," Fran said. "I didn't bring my key."

She had started to leave when Steve's SUV turned into Kelly Street. She was at the driver's door when it opened and Steve got out. Annette emerged from the passenger side.

"Hi, Fran," Steve greeted her. "Bonnie said you called. Sorry my cell wasn't working. Maybe the battery's out." He shot a look at Annette, and they both grinned.

Fran had a fair idea why she hadn't been able to reach either of them. She couldn't blame them, married just three months after eight years apart. But there was no time now for implausible explanations.

"Steve, where is Nell?"

"Mother's. Part of our campaign to get Nell and her grandmother to spend more time together, and Mrs. Grier promised brownies, so—"

"Fran?" Annette interrupted as she came around the front of the SUV. "What is it?"

Fran looked from one to the other. She didn't know how to make this easy or smooth. With Nell at Corbett House, *fast* was most important…unless Zach hadn't knocked on the door after all.

"Zach's here. He was heading for—"

"Zach?" Steve grabbed her arm, hard enough to hurt. "He's— Are you sure? Somebody who looked like him—after all these years—"

She answered the question he'd been afraid to ask ever since Zach left. "It's Zach. He's alive."

"Thank God." Annette's hands covered Steve's, easing his hold on Fran. Tears came into her eyes as she looked at her husband's face.

Fran wished she could let them feel the relief, and only the relief. Just for a little while. But there was no time.

"He was going to Corbett House, Steve. He was heading for the front door. I don't know if he made it, or if he left. But he might—"

Steve interrupted with one word. "Nell."

Zach contemplated the figure on the other side of Corbett House's front threshold. A girl with dark blond hair and intense blue eyes stood in the opening, looking him over.

He judged her age, based on height and weight, to be between eight and eleven. Probably the younger end of that scale. Countries where the nutrition wasn't as good, he'd have said older.

On a level untouched by professional training, he wondered what the hell a kid was doing in Corbett House. Lana had never particularly liked her own children, so why would she have this one around?

"Who are you?" he asked.

She glared. "I don't hafta tell you that. I don't hafta tell you anything. Who are you?"

He grinned. The kid had spirit, that was for sure. "Fair enough. I'm Zach—Zach Corbett."

"I've heard of you."

How could a kid this young sound so disapproving?

As fast as the question came, the answer formed. This was Tobias, Wisconsin, where the urge to gossip about the Corbetts was piped in along with the drinking water. Before he'd left he'd been the favorite Corbett to discuss. Sometimes he'd given people cause, sometimes they hadn't let facts stand in the way of a good story.

He gave the kid the cocky grin he'd used so often in Tobias. It felt a little rusty.

"Of course you've heard of me. I'm the no-good black sheep of the Corbetts and I used to live here." He looked past the kid into the wide hall with the polished wood stairway. He wasn't sure how much he could actually see of the dim interior, and how much came from memory. "A long, long time ago."

"Eight and a half years ago."

His gaze snapped back to the girl. Something in her voice sounded sharper than gossip, something personal.

"That's right. How'd you know that?"

"I know a lot of things. I know who you are. I've seen your picture. You left seven months before I was born—because I'm Nell Corbett. And you're my no-good black-sheep father."

Steve took off at a run on the most direct path to Corbett House.

Annette and Fran followed, but he'd already disappeared

inside the back door when they reached the steps. Annette stopped Fran with a hand on her arm.

"Does he know? Does Zach know about Nell?"

Nell, who had been told this past spring that Steve was not her biological father, as she had believed.

Nell, who had just started to fully absorb the knowledge that the man she'd never met but thought of as her Uncle Zach was her biological father.

Nell, who had come to Fran asking questions about Zach and Lily, her biological parents, because, as the child had said with concern, "I can't ask Dad and Annette or they might worry I don't want to be their daughter. I'm just curious."

But there was no *just* about her curiosity.

"I don't think so. He didn't... No. I'm sure. He doesn't know."

Annette sucked in a breath with a half-swallowed sob. A woman who feared for her family, because that's what Annette and Steve and Nell were—a family.

Fran stopped. She had no right to be part of this.

But at the top of the steps, Annette turned back. "Please." That was all she said, but Fran understood.

Annette was asking her not only to come in, to enter into what would be a tense, emotional family scene—even if Zach never found out Nell was his birth daughter, there were plenty of other currents running through the Corbett family—but also to do what she could to calm the waters.

As a lifelong friend and neighbor, while at the same time an outsider to the family, Fran might be able to help. She'd been told so many times how calm and peaceful she was to be around, she had accepted that it had to be the truth—no matter how uncalm and unpeaceful she might feel inside.

She fell in behind Annette as they entered the kitchen. Eyes wide, Mrs. Grier, Lana Corbett's housekeeper, silently directed them to the hallway door that still swung back and forth with the force of Steve's push.

Zach had changed. The cocky swagger was gone, and along with the filled-out shoulders there'd been a new groundedness to him. His family would see that, and that could change everything….

They reached the front foyer, and Fran's hopes evaporated.

"What does she mean I'm her father?" Zach demanded, looking at Steve.

Steve had his arm around Nell's shoulders, holding her against his side. Behind the defiance blazing out of Nell's blue eyes, so like Zach's, Fran also saw confusion. Nell squirmed—not away from Steve, but in front of him, still with his arm around her, so she could see everything that was going on except Steve's face. Which also meant Steve couldn't see his daughter's face.

Oh, yes, Nell was his daughter. Steve had been this girl's father from the day she was born, and he would be forever.

Annette stepped beside Steve, her arm against his, and Fran saw him shift his weight to deepen the contact. Even Lana, whose face seemed frozen in expressionless shock, stood beside Steve, though with a two-foot gap between her and her older son's family.

Opposite this family unit stood Zach, alone. His muscle-roped arms hung at his sides, his hands fisted.

Fran saw confusion in his blue eyes, too. An added uncertainty that hadn't been there when they had talked outside. Fran moved to the side, midway between him and his family.

"Nell is my daughter," Steve said. "Mine and Annette's."

"But she said—"

"Can't this wait?" Annette asked. A tear tracked down her cheek as she looked from her husband to his brother. She put her hand on Nell's shoulder, and Steve's hand covered hers there. "Zach's okay, and he's come back—let's enjoy that now."

But Fran could see that Steve's relief over his brother had been swamped by protectiveness of his daughter.

And Zach, staring back at Steve, wasn't going to let this go. He never had let anything go.

"Why would she think I'm her father?" he demanded.

"Because you are," Nell said. "You and Lily—"

"Quiet, Nell."

But Steve's order came too late. Zach had gone stone-still, confusion congealing into possibility. "Lily…"

They all knew he'd had a relationship with Lily Wilbanks before he'd left town. Lily had been Steve's high-school girlfriend. But by college, Steve and Annette were together and planning to marry, and Lily had set her sights on Zach, until he'd had a climactic fight with his mother and zoomed out of town on his motorcycle that long-ago spring.

Zach shifted his stance, like a boxer trying to regain his footing after a blow. "So Lily can clear this up, and—"

"Lily died more than six years ago," Steve said. "I'm the father on Nell's birth certificate, I've been her father since the moment she was born and I'm raising her, so you don't have to worry about any of it. You've let us know you're alive, and we're glad for that, but you can walk away now without any—"

"I'm not walking away until—"

"You did it before, you can do it again."

"Until," Zach picked up grimly, "I know what's going on here."

"It's none of your business." Steve's hold on Nell tightened.

"This is *my* family. You left and chose not to have anything more to do with this family."

Fran saw the vein at Zach's temple jump, as if touched by a live wire. But his voice was steady.

"The girl said I'm her father. Is she lying?"

Steve's silence answered eloquently.

"That makes it my damned business," Zach said. "I'm not going anywhere until I get some answers."

The two brothers, polar opposites when they'd been growing up, stared at each other with eerily similar carved-in-granite expressions.

"We don't have to do this now," Annette said. "We can talk tomorrow. Let's all take tonight to…adjust. That is, if you weren't planning on leaving Tobias right away, Zach."

"I'm staying," he said, not looking away from Steve. Fran wondered if anyone else noticed that his answer sidestepped any indication of what his original plan had been.

"You won't stay in this house, Zachary."

Fran flinched at Lana's clipped, cold voice, the first words she'd heard Lana say to her younger son. Zach showed no reaction.

"No problem," he said. "I can find a room at—"

"He can stay with me," Fran heard herself say calmly. "I have plenty of room."

Chapter Two

"I'm not going to stay here without paying rent."

Stopping on the staircase's bottom step, Fran looked over her shoulder to find that Zach had advanced exactly one pace past the front threshold of her house before making that proclamation. He held the door open with one hand on the knob. Poised for departure.

"That's absurd," she said. "All I'm giving you is a bed that's otherwise going to waste. There are four empty bedrooms and enough space in this place for you and me and three more people to rattle around in."

He gave her a look that was in some language she couldn't translate—possibly male.

"I'm not staying here without paying rent."

Make that language stubborn male. Specifically, stubborn male intent on focusing on something—anything—other than the reason he was staying at all.

She turned to face him fully, but didn't descend the step. Better to deal with him at eye-level than look up.

She should have remembered his stubbornness before she'd made her spur-of-the-moment offer. Great time to take the plunge into impulsiveness, Fran.

"No handouts, Fran," he added, as if he thought she intended the offer of a room to make up for that moment in Corbett House's front hall.

Zach hadn't gotten any farther inside his childhood home than the front hall.

You won't stay in this house, Zachary.

God, she'd wanted to shake Lana Corbett. Annette had looked stricken, Nell seemed even more confused, and Steve, as focused as he was on Nell, had winced.

Zach had given no reaction at all.

It was as if he'd expected his mother's response. But he couldn't have, or he wouldn't have come back. Would he?

"Being neighborly is not a handout," Fran told him. "Besides, how long could you afford to sit here in Tobias and pay out rent?"

That hit something in him she didn't quite understand. Perhaps it was the prospect of an extended stay in Tobias, but maybe more.

"I'm not going to be here forever. As soon as I figure out what the hell is happening and what to do about it, I'll be gone."

"And you think that the best resolution to a situation that's developed over all these years is going to happen at the snap of your fingers? Think again, Zach Corbett."

She half expected him to spout off or to take off. He did neither. He dragged in a slow, deep breath, as if his stubbornness shifted to a lower gear, the kind designed to drag him up a mountain if necessary.

"I appreciate your offering me a place, Fran, but I'm not going to stay here on your charity. I'd get a job if I had to—"

"Fine," she said crisply. His stubbornness and his pride. Even as a girl she'd seen the trouble that pair had gotten him into. She'd also wondered if they had saved him from being crushed.

From her childhood observation post, surrounded by the security of her loving parents, she'd watched the inhabitants of Corbett House next door and wondered why people were the way they were. Early on she'd come to the conclusion that being a Corbett required certain attributes. Wimps need not apply.

"This isn't ingratitude or—" Zach sounded defensive.

"I said fine." Because what was the alternative? Like he might back down? Besides, she had an idea. "So, do you want to work for your bread and board?"

He looked around the hallway, assessing. That gaze had a gloss of expertise about it. Maybe he worked in construction.

That errant thought rocked her—like dozing in the passenger seat of a car until it stops with a slight jolt that brings you wide awake, and you have no idea where you are.

What had he been doing during his years away? In all the emotions of his return, no one had thought to ask.

And he hadn't said.

In fact, she realized, he had offered not one word about what he'd done or who he'd become since the spring day he'd shouted defiance at his mother, revved his motorcycle across Corbett House's pristine front lawn and ridden due west.

"Doesn't look like you need any work done," he said. "The place is in great shape."

In other words, don't make up work for me. Oh, yes, stubbornness and pride.

She knew better than to dent the one if she hoped to soften up the other.

"That's because Rob beat you to it."

His brows lifted. "Rob's in Tobias? When you said it was the two of you, you meant living here? I was sure he'd be some big financial whiz."

"He was. Now...he'll be moving to Tobias permanently at some point. But he's going to be in Chicago for a while, at least during the week. It's a long story. Let's settle this first. I don't need work on the house, but I do have a job for you, if you want it."

"As long as I'm staying in your house, I'll do whatever work you say. But I'm going to take care of this as fast as I can. Don't count on me for something long-term."

She didn't argue again about how long it would take him to sort out the issues with his family; she responded only to his warning. "I won't count on you for anything long-term."

A flicker of something rose in his eyes, then subsided as quickly. He produced a twisted grin.

"Pure Fran Dalton. Cut to the chase, even if it draws blood." Before she decided whether that called for an answer, he continued, "What's the job?"

"I'm in charge of renovating the gardens at Bliss House. I could use someone with muscles." Now why on earth had she said that? She hurried on, hoping the heat she felt pushing up her throat would turn back south without revealing itself on her face. "And if I could find someone who can run one of those small front-end loaders, I'd be forever grateful because I could stop begging the construction crew for favors. I don't suppose you can run one of those?"

"Enough to get by."

He said it with low-key assurance, as if Zach Corbett, a member of the richest and most influential family in Tobias and—more to the point—the son of Lana Corbett, would naturally know how to use blue-collar machinery. The town had nearly imploded from the tut-tutting when he'd gotten a motorcycle. At least that was certified bad-boy-toy material—but a front-end loader?

When she didn't speak, he asked, "What's the deal with Bliss House's gardens being renovated? Miss Trudi...?"

"Miss Trudi's fine. But the situation with Bliss House is another long story. It'll be easier to show you and then fill in the gaps. I'll take you up to your room and we can go over to Bliss House after you've settled in."

He didn't move.

She held up her right hand. "I swear, I will extract every penny's worth of room and board from you by working you to the bone."

One side of his mouth twitched and mischief sparkled in those famed blue eyes.

"Not for board, you won't. I'll buy my own share of groceries. And do my share of the cooking."

She raised her hands, then let them fall against her sides in surrender.

"Great. Perfect. However you want it. Can we please go upstairs now?"

Grinning, he said, "No. I've gotta go get the car and my things. I'll be right back."

Still standing on the stairs, she watched him through the three windows at the top of the front door as he followed the walkway to the sidewalk. No, he definitely didn't swagger anymore. Yet that walk couldn't have belonged to anyone else in the world.

He'd left his car somewhere and walked up the hill to Corbett House. Why? Why not drive up to it? Had he considered walking past without going in, without being seen? But surely that would be easier to do driving a car?

She shook her head. Foolishness. She could stand here until next week guessing at reasons, and what difference would it make? None. He was here, and she should deal with what needed to be done.

Upstairs, she put out fresh towels and necessities. She kept clean sheets on the beds—never knew when someone might need a place to stay.

"Fran?" Zach called from the top of the stairs.

She stuck her head out of the guest room at the far end of the hall, the opposite end from Corbett House. He stood in a pool of light from the hall window, so bright that for an instant he seemed to shimmer, like a ghost of his past self.

"Down here," she said. He started toward her.

"Is your room down the other end still? Looking out at Corbett House?" He carried one bag, similar to a gym bag, with an unfamiliar insignia on it. That was all he'd brought?

"Yes."

"Are you putting me at this end because you want privacy or to spare my feelings from having to look out on the old homestead where I'm no longer welcomed?"

Something else that hadn't changed. Zach never used social amnesia to smooth over uncomfortable facts, such as his being turned away at Corbett House.

"Both."

She stepped back to let him precede her into the room.

"The bathroom's there." She pointed unnecessarily through

the open door on the south wall. "The bathroom also opens to another guest room, but with that one empty, you'll have all the privacy you could want."

Having pointed out towels, toiletries and extra blankets, she said she'd be downstairs when he was ready, and retreated.

She did not want to watch him pull out the few belongings that could reside in that small bag.

She poured herself a glass of lemonade and went to sit on the porch.

Nell needed time and exposure to Zach so she could know him as a real person, not the mythical outlaw-cum-hero uncle of her imagination and not whatever form he'd taken in her fertile mind since she'd been told that Zach, not Steve, was her biological father.

In the end, doing what was best for Nell had to be best for Steve and Annette, too. Working things out now, no matter how painful, had to be better for their little family than pretending the past had never happened. They knew that, too; that was why they'd told Nell the truth.

Fran had thought them wise and brave when they'd told Nell the truth. She trusted in their wisdom and bravery to reach a good resolution now. But they needed time. Time to get over the shock, time to find their way.

To give everyone that time, Zach had to stay.

That's why she'd offered the room.

Not from any heartbreak over a prodigal being unwelcome in his home.

This house hadn't changed much, either.

It was the kind of house where clean curtains fluttered in summer breezes and there was always lemonade in the fridge or hot chocolate on the stove. He'd had his share of both here.

Not that he'd be around this time to hit hot-chocolate weather.

No matter what Fran said about not being able to resolve things in the snap of his fingers, he knew how fast information could be gathered, how quickly a situation could be assessed and a decision made. If it had to be.

From the bottom of the stairs he followed the center hall to the large open room across the back of the house. Vicki Dalton had been ahead of her time when she'd had doorways widened to generous arches and replaced a wall with a pass-through. The result was that instead of a small, closed-up kitchen, breakfast area and family room, there was a free-flowing space where the Daltons had done most of their living…and dying.

Vicki's days had ended on a hospital bed in the family-room area, set up so she could look out through the porch to the trees and gardens she'd loved. Had Dennis Dalton done the same with his daughter at his side?

That was pure Fran, right down to her toes. Zach bet she'd made a good nurse, too. Calm, unflappable, but with plenty of spark behind the no-nonsense.

But why did Fran remain in this house where she felt she was *rattling* around? Why hadn't she moved on after her father died? Gotten on with her own life? And for God's sake, junked those clothes that Miss Trudi would have considered old-fashioned when she was a girl.

Fran must have heard him come downstairs because she walked in from the porch, carrying an empty glass. She gave it a little lift, offering him one. He shook his head.

The screen door swung fast behind her. To keep it from slamming she gave a stutter step to catch the screen with her backside, then stepped forward, letting the door close softly.

She did it automatically, with the unselfconsciousness of an ingrained habit.

Her movement reminded him of the sight of that backside with the tan jeans snugged over it as she crouched in the flower bed. And he had an automatic response, too.

God, what an asshole. Returning to Tobias for the first time in years, letting his family know he wasn't dead, and discovering he had a daughter—that wasn't enough for him? No, he had to lust after the kindhearted neighbor girl.

Woman, his libido amended.

He pivoted and latched on to the first thing in sight.

"What the hell is all this? It looks like… That's Bliss House."

He walked to the table where the Dalton family had eaten most of their meals, now covered with stacks of books and folders, forming occasional mountains above a plain of photos and papers.

Photos displayed the old mansion as he remembered it from growing up. But others appeared to date from shortly after it had been built in the late 1800s. While Corbett House was the picture of decorum, Bliss House displayed an exuberant eccentricity, just like the branch of the Corbett family that had built it. Zach slid one photo aside and came across another of the same area. A recent shot, with construction scaffolding and bushes wrapped in protective netting.

"These are some of my materials on the gardens."

"Some?" He circled the table, picking up a folder, a list, a book, putting each back in place. "Must be one hell of a job to need all this."

"It is."

"Who took these?" He tapped a trio of photos, blown up and mounted on poster board, that were lined up on the buffet against the wall, along with a copy of an old-fashioned garden plan. He squinted at a view looking down on tangled, wild grounds beyond a cleared circle around the house.

"I did. Shortly after I agreed to oversee the work on the gardens."

Judging from the angle and his memory of Bliss House… "From the roof?"

"Yes."

"Damn it, Fran, that roof wasn't safe a decade ago. I can't imagine it's any better now. That—"

"The scaffolding that Max Trevetti's construction crew was using was already set up, so I had that."

Max Trevetti? Annette's older brother? Zach remembered him—a man when Zach was still a boy. Max was several years older than Annette, who was Zach's age. Since when was Fran friendly with Max?

He shook his head. "Construction scaffolding's dangerous, Fran."

She gave him a look that clearly said, who was he to talk about danger to her? And she was right. The Zach she'd known would have done cartwheels on that roof if he'd thought of it.

He let it drop.

"Why did you want the pictures so bad?"

"To spot ghost marks from the original garden. Indentations that show where a path was or built-up areas of old beds. Things like that."

She had books on plants, landscape design and Wisconsin horticulture. Catalogs from heritage flower, vegetable, herb, shrub and tree growers, stacks of what appeared to be research, an open binder with receipts, another with a diagram that sported snakes of sticky-notes.

"Looks like you could track down any garden ghosts in a three-state area with all this."

"I've let it spread as we get into the late stages," she said. "I'm heading over to the gardens soon. I need to check some plants that I couldn't get to earlier because Max's men were in that area. So I came home to tackle the bed out front when... Well, you don't care about all that. I'm going back to Bliss House, and if you'd like to come, I can give you an overview before you start work tomorrow."

"I'm not committing to anything until I've talked to Steve."

"You can safely plan on working tomorrow, Zach. You're going to be here for a few days anyway. You can't go marching over to their house, not with Nell all ears. And Steve and Annette need to talk with Nell and to each other before they talk to you. You're going to have to be patient. And flexible."

She'd said the words *patient* and *flexible* with an emphasis that made it seem as though they had special meaning.

"Plus, life goes on," she added. "There's Nell's school schedule and Steve's job and their work with Bliss House—we're gearing up for the opening in three weeks. You can't walk back in after eight and a half years and expect everyone to drop their lives to sort this out."

At least not tonight. Absently, he picked a book up off the sideboard. "Okay, I'll go with you."

"That's not..."

She let the words die without telling him what the book wasn't. He'd already seen what it was.

Childish but firm handwriting on the front flyleaf declared it the property of Nell Corbett, Third Grade, Mrs. Peaslen's Class.

Holding this book, seeing the handwriting there made it all real.

Lily had been pregnant with his baby when he'd left Tobias. Somehow Steve had come to raise that baby.

Lily had died. About six years ago, Steve had said. But Steve had also said he was listed as the father on the birth certificate. How did that happen? A baby, now a girl, who stared at him with blue eyes that looked as if they could cut through reinforced concrete.

His daughter.

God almighty, his daughter.

"Let's go, Zach. The days are already getting shorter and—"

"Sit down. I have questions first."

She remained standing. "You're going to have to get the answers from your family, Zach. I offered you a place to stay because you all need to deal with this, but I am not going to get in the middle of it. You have to talk to each other. I'm going to Bliss House now."

She walked to the porch door, holding it open.

He put the book down and followed.

Muted but high-pitched sounds made him peer into a shadowed area of the porch. Inside a low, carpeted box, a large, fluffy dog lay on her side with small, squirming forms clambering around her.

"This is Chester," Fran said.

"Chester? You named a female dog Chester?"

"I didn't. Kay did."

"Kay?"

"Rob's fiancé. She's with Rob in Chicago and his building doesn't allow dogs."

"What's going on with Rob in Chicago?"

She huffed out a breath. "Zach, we'll be here forever if you expect me to catch you up on everything that's happened since you left. Eight and a half years is a long time."

"What if my questions are about you?"

That wasn't fair, because the questions he really wanted to ask were about his daughter. He wanted Fran to describe every detail of Nell Corbett's life—yesterday, then the day before, and the day before that, and every day before that, right back to her birth. And before her birth. To try to figure this whole thing out.

God. He had a daughter.

"Then you must be looking for boring answers," Fran said.

"Don't sell yourself short, Fran." He realized his survey of her curves had become a little too appreciative when her cheeks pinkened. She wasn't flustered—he couldn't remember ever seeing Fran flustered—but she was pink nonetheless. The most matter-of-fact blusher he'd ever seen.

So maybe he hadn't lied. Maybe he had questions about Fran after all.

She snorted a laugh. "If you're reduced to practicing your wiles on me, Zach, you're in a hard way. I'm going. Make up your mind if you're coming with or staying here."

He didn't catch up with her until she'd reached her car, parked in the two-car driveway behind the house. She might have wondered if he'd debated staying. But his slow start had a different cause.

If you're reduced to practicing your wiles on me, Zach, you're in a hard way.

He got in the passenger side. The car had been closed up, holding the sun's heat. But this was late September in Wisconsin, so the heat wasn't stifling. Still, it held a closeness that intensified an aroma mixed of sweet earthiness and fresh lemons.

Fran. He had the strongest urge to stretch across the seat and bury his face in her hair.

He jabbed the button to open his window.

"That's Steve and Annette's house."

She'd backed the car out of the drive and pointed across Kelly Street. Kelly divided the backyards of the five large houses facing Lakeview on one side from modest suburban houses nestled among big trees on the other.

"Steve bought the house when he and Nell came back to Tobias, when he was hired as town manager."

Zach leaned forward, looking out the windshield at the neat Cape Cod with a girl's bicycle at the side of the driveway. He continued looking, tracking through the driver's open window and the backseat window as Fran drove slowly down the street.

Steve was living here? Practically in Corbett House's backyard? Why? He could have gotten away and he hadn't—

Or maybe his brother couldn't have gotten away because Steve had been raising Zach's child. Maybe he'd needed help raising a baby. Though God knew Lana wouldn't have been much help.

"How the hell did this happen?"

A faint, wry smile touched Fran's lips. "You would know that better than I would, Zach."

He liked that she didn't pretend not to know what he'd meant, but impatience still came through when he said, "Steve having the girl, I mean."

"That's something you should discuss with Steve. He's the only one who knows the whole story."

"But you know some of it."

"Yes, I know some of it."

"And you're not telling me."

She didn't try to dodge the accusation, she didn't even squirm. She stopped at a stop sign, looked him straight in the eye and said, "No, I'm not telling you. This is one thing you need to deal with yourself."

With the possibility of getting his answers from her removed, his single-minded focus widened enough that he belatedly could see the humor in her comment about his being in a better position to know—how Lily had become pregnant, anyway—than her. He could also feel the bite in her last comment. *This is one thing you need to deal with yourself.*

That was Fran, all right—cut to the chase and cut to the bone.

"Ah, yes," he said. "Zach Corbett, famed throughout Tobias for not dealing with things himself."

She shrugged and eased the car forward. "You tended to get into things and then not finish them. And—"

"Are you still holding a grudge for that lemonade stand when we were six?"

"I was six. You were seven. And I lost a month's allowance buying all the supplies for the 'best lemonade stand ever,' if I remember your quote. Then when we sold only two cups—both to my mother—you took off."

"Led astray by an older man, huh? Bet that never happened to you again. You should thank me."

"No, that never happened again."

Something in her words made him study her profile. It was as calm and smooth as the words. But it was distant, contained—definitely not open to the public.

Fran had always been quiet. As a careless boy he'd thought her timid. As a teenager he hadn't thought about her much at all, because she had definitely not been a prospective conquest.

Now…now, he wondered. That's all. Wondered.

Zach whistled an amazed acknowledgement as she drove past the gleaming wrought-iron gate flanked by power-washed and repainted brick walls at the front entrance to the grounds of Bliss House. The gate gave tantalizing glimpses of the house's white facade.

Hearing that whistle, Fran felt fully justified in taking the slight detour that gave him the full impact of the renovations. She'd hoped it would take his mind off waiting for answers.

Okay, maybe she also wanted a *ta-da!* moment of showing off what the Bliss House committee, along with Trevetti Building's construction crew and volunteers, had achieved.

"I can't believe it," Zach said. "I remember a place that looked like it might sink into the ground any second."

"And you didn't see it at its worst. Miss Trudi simply couldn't take care of it—not physically and not financially. But no one could get through to her that she needed help, not for the longest time. Annette and Steve together finally had to lay it on the line—she could lose Bliss House and her independence for good if she didn't let some of us help her."

"How was she going to lose her independence?"

She spoke carefully. "Some people in the community believed that Miss Trudi would be better off in a retirement home and Tobias would be better off without Bliss House."

Zach faced her and said one word: "Lana."

Either she hadn't been oblique enough, Fran thought, or he knew his mother quite well, even after this time apart.

"Yes." No sense sugarcoating it. She doubted Zach would buy it anyway. "She headed a group that was pushing to tear down Bliss House, with plans to develop the site."

He cursed under his breath. "Some concrete block devoted to making even more money she didn't need."

"I don't know the details." From what she'd heard, he was close, but she could see no good coming from confirming his worst opinions of Lana. "But with Annette and Steve leading the way, people came together and got behind this alternative solution for Miss Trudi and Bliss House."

"Steve's got Annette doing the Corbett duty thing in looking after the town, huh?"

She stopped in the drive and gave him a level look. "There is nothing wrong with wanting to help your town. And in this case, it's Steve's job. As I told you, he's town manager—actually the whole county."

"So he never became a lawyer like Lana planned?"

"No."

She watched another piece click into the new vision he was forming of his family.

"Steve's led Tobias in a real upswing," she said over the top of the car as they closed their respective doors. She pulled her work gloves from a back pocket. "If you go to the lakeside—"

"I saw. Moved the pier. Buildings spruced up. New businesses. It cleaned up nice. That's Steve's work?"

"Yes. He brought in more jobs, too. But some of the older people could use financial help and others need to work at home. The crafts center at Bliss House will let them sell what they already make. Plus, it'll bring more visitors to town."

She led him down the drive that curved between the brick wall that enclosed Miss Trudi's domain and a low wall that set off the patio outside the main house. Workers could be seen inside through windows that still wore manufacturers' stickers.

"So show me these gardens you've been working on so hard."

"It's not a precise re-creation, of course."

"You're kidding. With all that stuff you have, I'd think you were intending to put back every blade of grass."

She made a face at him. "Hardly. For one thing, we didn't

want to take down mature trees, which we'd have to do to qualify as restoring or reconstructing. The trees the Bliss family planted would have been young in 1890. The elms—" she swept her arm toward the entryway from the street "—can't be replaced and the drive needs to be wider, so we'll have planter boxes on the brick wall. We can change those seasonally, and they'll provide visual interest. It's like what we're doing with the house—adapting what's historical to modern use.

"Miss Trudi's quarters being enclosed makes the whole design different, too." She gestured to the miniature compound where Max and his workers had converted and connected several old outbuildings to create a safe and modern home for Miss Trudi.

"Originally there was a conservatory with exotic plants, but there's no way we can afford that yet. In fact, we can't afford many of the specimen plants I'd like." She sighed. "Most of the paths are in. Ghost marks of their design showed up on those photos I took, and once I got in among the plants, I could really see the original design."

He touched a finger to a healing scratch on her forearm. The scratch abruptly burned even more than it had when she'd done it.

"Looks like you've been getting into the plants too much, Fran. But what I'm wondering is what I'm going to do to earn my keep? You've got most of it finished."

"We have trees and shrubs arriving next week. And then we have very special trees being delivered. All of them must be planted."

"Special trees?"

She ignored the lilt of mockery in the question. Or was it amusement?

"A descendent of Bliss House's original head gardener has

trees on her family's property descended from the maples planted in the four corners of the grounds here. She's offered to donate several. We can't afford to move a huge one, but we're going to take a five-inch diameter tree to plant in place of the one corner tree that's died, then two smaller ones."

"Doesn't sound bad. I can get that done tomorrow."

"No, you can't."

That stubborn glint in his eyes intensified.

She held up a hand. "You can't go charging in, Zach. There's a lot going on here and we have a daily schedule worked out right up to the opening in less than three weeks. If you're serious about working for your room, you'll do things when I say. If you can't take orders…"

He leaned back, examining her. She wanted to squirm, to turn away, to do anything but stand still and firm. She stood still and firm.

"I can take orders," he said. This tone she truly couldn't interpret. Not stubborn exactly. There was some pride, but not on the surface. "If they're reasonable," he added.

"I'm always reasonable."

He laughed. Not the throw-back-his-head-and-let-it-all-out laughter she remembered from a young Zach, but the first undampened amusement he'd shown since he'd walked up the sidewalk earlier this afternoon.

The thing was, it was the plain truth. She was reasonable right to her core. Reason and calm—those were Fran Dalton's strengths. Everyone knew that. And she'd learned the penalty for straying from those strengths.

"So what've you got to keep me busy until these trees and shrubs get delivered?"

She smiled. "Oh, I'll keep you busy. We're going to be planting many smaller plants, as well as bulbs for next spring.

The Garden Club ladies have generously volunteered to help, but I don't think seven women pushing seventy or more can handle the volume. We have an order of nearly four hundred tulip bulbs coming because they'll provide such dramatic color the first season and—"

"Okay, okay, so you do need me."

Chapter Three

It was windy. The kind of wind Zach associated with Wisconsin. A straightforward blow from west to east. No fancy shifts and swirls.

It almost took the weed out of Fran's gloved hand as she straightened from plucking the interloper from underneath a bush she informed him was a *viburnum carlcephalum*.

Having nearly completed their circuit of Bliss House, with Fran explaining Victorians' gardening likes and dislikes all the way around, they were in a back corner with a couple of empty raised beds in the middle and a line of bushes around the outside.

He could have told her to point him to where she wanted a plant stuck and he'd get it done, but it seemed rude to interrupt her enthusiasm. Besides, she was fun to watch, with her face all serious while her hands drew patterns in the air.

Not to mention his enjoyment when she bent over the way

she'd just done to snag an errant weed. Now that was definitely worth watching.

"Bliss House originally would have had a much larger kitchen garden to supply the household all year round, as well as herbs for medical purposes. Not to mention fruit trees and shrubs. But the flower gardens will draw more visitors. So the kitchen garden's a sample of what they would have had. We dug out most of the raspberry, currant and blueberry bushes."

"So there's no more work to be done with them, right?"

She gave him a quizzical look, apparently catching something in his tone. "That's right."

"Good. Because that's one thing I won't do. Nothing to do with raspberry bushes."

Her brows rose. "Are you allergic?"

"No. The berries are fine. It's the bushes."

He watched a slow shifting of her face, her cheeks lifting, her lips curving, and then all the changes resolving into a grin. A genuine face-shifting, sassy-as-hell grin.

"You're afraid of raspberry bushes? Zach Corbett is afraid of raspberry bushes?"

"Not afraid," he said with dignity. "A healthy respect, combined with a desire to keep my digits and limbs attached and not get sliced to bits. You know that expression about death by a thousand cuts? That's really about raspberry bushes."

"But…you and Steve and Rob used to go raspberry-picking as kids. Rob's talked about that—riding your bikes over to that thicket by the river, and eating raspberries until you were stuffed."

"Yeah. Well, guess who got to do most of the picking because he was the smallest and supposedly could fit in better? I used to get pretty damned torn up." A faint grin touched his lips. "Along with my clothes."

"So they picked on the youngest, huh? Then why did you keep going?"

"Because they were the big kids. I had to keep up and I had to pick the raspberries—those were the conditions before I could go."

"Aw, poor Zach." Her grin stayed sassy.

"That's right," he said, deadpan. "Finally someone realizes it. Folks thought being me was an easy gig, but there were definitely drawbacks to growing up Zach Corbett of Corbett House."

He'd expected more teasing for his poor-pitiful-me tone. Instead, she said, without an ounce of pity, "I know."

She made it such clear-eyed fact that an urge to tell her— tell her about his leaving Tobias, what he'd been doing and why he'd come back—hung in his mind like a bright balloon.

"Besides," he said, letting the balloon drift away on the breeze, "coming home after raspberry-picking with my clothes and me all torn up drove Lana wild."

The wind swept the loose tendrils of Fran's hair back, pressed her clothes against her body. She reached to tuck a vine into a trellis, and the fabric of her jeans plastered her calves and stretched taut over the long curve of her thighs. The tail of her shirt flipped up, revealing a flat stomach and a tiny triangle of pale skin above her waist. Across her ribs, the shirt flattened, then swelled with the curve of her breasts, defining their full outline as clearly as a sheet might to a lover's eyes.

And then she went after another weed. This time she didn't crouch, but bent from her waist to reach over a bushy plant and grab the tall weed behind it. The position pulled those tan jeans tight over a firm rump stuck up in the air.

He swore to himself. Under those utilitarian work clothes,

Fran Dalton had the kind of body that men who weren't into sticks dreamed about. When the hell had that happened?

"What?" she demanded, half resigned, half belligerent.

With her backside still in the air, she was looking over her shoulder at him.

Only then did he realize he'd emitted a low whistle.

"When did you change?"

Fran partially straightened. In an effort to avoid the dirt caking her work gloves, she used her forearm to push her hair off her face, but she left a smear along her temple anyway.

"Change? How?"

"You used to be, uh, chubby. You're not now."

She straightened the rest of the way quickly, her cheeks tinged pink, and he didn't think it was all from the position she'd been in.

"College." She moved down the path ahead of him, keeping her gaze on the plants.

"Most people gain weight at college."

She shrugged. "I'd been cooking for Dad and Rob, and keeping up with them at the table. When I went to school I wasn't around food all the time and I didn't have a couple of hollow-legged males to feed."

He wondered, as he watched the breeze ruffle her hair over the smudge, if it had been as simple as she made it sound.

"Now what?" she asked, hands on hips.

He'd been staring at her.

Without answering, he closed the distance between them. Her expression didn't change. It should have. She should have registered an awareness, a recognition of the potential intent of any sane male of a certain age who crossed into the personal space of a woman like her. She should have registered wariness. But not Fran Dalton.

Maybe that's what spurred him to his next move.

He cupped the back of her head in his large left palm, feeling the heat of the sun on the soft surface of her hair, and the cool of the coming night in the depths below.

There, now her expression changed. But not to awareness or wariness. Surprise—yes, that was there. But more than that, confusion.

She still didn't get the potential?

With his one hand holding her head, he touched the side of his other thumb to the center of her lips, then traced their outline with deliberation. Up from the dip in the center of her top lip, then down the gentle slope to the corner, where it tucked in, across the wide straight line of her bottom lip—no pouting here—to the opposite corner, up the corresponding slope of her top lip and home once more to that decided dip in the center. Temptation whispered to repeat the circuit. Slower, softer.

He jerked his hand up, using his thumb to catch the smudge near her temple and transfer the dirt from her fair, smooth skin onto skin still nicked and scratched.

He released her abruptly and stepped back.

"There," he said, holding out his dirtied thumb as proof of what, exactly, he didn't know. "That's what."

"Oh." Her fingers went to her temple—not her lips, her temple—and rubbed. "Thanks."

She didn't know.

God, the woman didn't know. Not what her body could do to a man, and not how to read the signs. It was a dangerous ignorance. Dangerous for men who might care about her. And dangerous for her if she encountered men who didn't care about her.

Motion to the side caught his attention.

And there stood Miss Trudi Bliss, her hair grayer, but the purple smock, loose pants and tennis shoes eerily familiar, watching him with great interest.

Following the direction of his gaze, Fran turned, too. "Miss Trudi, good afternoon. Did you know Zach's back?"

"Zach! How wonderful to see you!" the old woman said, as if she'd just spotted him. Removing gardening gloves nearly as dirty as Fran's, she stepped around a gray cat and advanced quickly to throw her arms around him, hitting not far above his waist because of the differences in their heights, and leaving him to wrap his arms around her sloping shoulders.

He squeezed her, surprising himself. She'd been a tartar his entire childhood, yet he felt a well of affection for this distant relative—a great-aunt with some removes thrown in if he remembered Lana's lectures on genealogy, which he'd tried his best not to.

The feeling of affection ebbed somewhat when Miss Trudi released him from the hug, but reached up and laid her palm along his cheek. From another angle it might have appeared to be a sweet gesture of welcome. But even if he hadn't felt the decided firmness of the hold, he found himself directly in the line of fire of her sharp, searching eyes.

Miss Trudi patted his cheek with more muscle than necessary. "I am glad to see that you have come home finally, Zach."

"I haven't—"

"You are taller than when you left."

"Yeah. But I haven't come back for good. Just visiting."

"And you chose to come to see me? I am touched, Zach. However, you do have obligations and issues awaiting you elsewhere in Tobias that are of more import than visiting me."

"Zach's going to stay awhile in Tobias," Fran said before he could answer. "That's why we're here. He insists he wants to work while he stays at the house, and we certainly can use help with the planting."

Miss Trudi looked from him to Fran. He didn't doubt for a moment that she'd put together the pieces with fair accuracy—that he hadn't been invited to stay at Corbett House and wouldn't have accepted if he had been, and that Fran's generosity had provided the solution.

When Miss Trudi's gaze returned to him, Zach had the oddest flash of having a target painted on his chest. Which was nonsense. Considering what he faced with his immediate family, what could Miss Trudi possibly do to him?

"What a splendid idea, Fran," the older woman said. "You most certainly do need assistance, and Zach is the perfect solution. Oh!" She gave a theatrical start. "That is if Zach is willing and able to do such hard physical labor. I seem to remember that as a boy he…" She fluttered a vague hand.

"Was a lazy good-for-nothing?" Zach asked pleasantly.

"Precisely." Miss Trudi smiled broadly, as if he'd gotten the correct answer on a pop quiz.

"I can do the work. And I will. Besides, it seems to me that's Fran's concern, not yours."

"Miss Trudi's on the committee, too, and Bliss House is still her home—"

"You said she sold it to the town." Zach cut across Fran's words. "And you pointed out her new home on the way. You're in charge of the gardens. Nobody else."

If he'd hoped to rattle Miss Trudi—and to be honest, he didn't know exactly what his goal had been in that little speech—he failed.

"Indeed, Fran is the heart and soul of the gardens," Miss

Trudi agreed. "Without her vision and dedication, there would be no gardens."

"That's not true, Miss Trudi. Suz had the idea to restore the gardens and your ancestor had the vision for the design."

"Ideas and designs are all well and good, but you have expanded upon them and implemented them beautifully."

"Oh, I'm not saying I haven't done anything—I'm not that modest," Fran said with a laugh. "But I know my limitations."

"It has been my experience that what an individual considers her limitations are, in fact, brakes she applies when she could be gathering momentum."

Fran appeared slightly taken aback by Miss Trudi's declaration, but Zach didn't have time to observe her for more than a second before his distant relative pulled in a breath and turned to him.

"Regardless of the level of credit Fran deserves for this enterprise, it is fortuitous that you have returned at this moment to help her. Your return at any time would, of course, be celebrated. This adds a fillip to the delight."

His mouth twisted. "I suspect the rest of the Corbetts won't be celebrating with you or experiencing any fillips of delight."

"Nonsense. Your whereabouts and welfare have never been far from anyone's mind."

"Yeah? Well, now that they know I'm alive, I suspect they'd prefer I returned to where I came from."

"Ah. And where is it that you came from, Zach?"

"Virginia."

"Virginia?" Fran said. "Really? You went west that day, and I suppose I envisioned you in the west."

"I was there awhile. You could say I've been working my way around the world and I've gotten as far as Virginia."

Miss Trudi beamed. "But now you're home."

"I told you, this isn't a permanent situation, Miss Trudi. I was going to stop by and…" And what? He hadn't known what he'd intended to do. He created a grin. "Say hello."

"Yet you have decided to remain for a time that requires you to stay with our Fran and to pay your way. Why?"

He flashed a look at Fran. Did Miss Trudi not know…? But Fran's head was bent in apparent fascinated study of her shoes. The beat-up walking shoes weren't worth that much interest.

"Family complications," he said, repeating the phrase he'd used on the phone when he'd called Taz from Fran's guest room earlier.

His urban search-and-rescue-team supervisor had said, "I told you before, take a month. You've got that time and more coming."

Miss Trudi said, "Ah, you refer to Nell."

"Not sure I follow, Miss Trudi."

She slapped him on his arm with her gardening gloves. The woman didn't know her strength. Instead of a mild reprimand, it stung, as well as leaving a streak of dirt on his shirt. Since he'd packed for only a couple days away, he couldn't afford extracurricular dirt.

"Do not prevaricate, young man. You most certainly do follow. You are Nell's biological father. And since Steve and Annette told her the truth of her birth, she is aware of that fact."

"Okay, so Nell confided in you—"

"Oh, my dear Zach." She smiled with warm indulgence. "I have known from the time that Lily's condition became apparent."

"How could you?"

"That is irrelevant now, is it not? Yes, I was certain you would agree. The only issue that matters is what you are going to do now that *you* know."

She waited, as if she expected him to spout off a detailed plan. Hell, even when you trained and planned and practiced, you could come up against situations where you had to improvise. For this situation he didn't have any of that—not tools, not training, not plans. Nothing.

"I'm going to assess the setup and then...and then we'll see."

At the house, Zach excused himself to make a phone call upstairs while Fran checked the heating-pad setting that kept the whelping box warm enough for the puppies.

Chester was still focused primarily on her puppies, born almost two weeks earlier. But Fran could see her starting to venture away a little. Chester even came to her and nudged her hand to be petted.

But when Zach returned fifteen minutes later, Chester positioned herself between him and the puppies.

"Zach, there's something I'd like to ask you."

"Shoot."

"You do realize that it will come out—about you and Lily and Nell. A story like that can't be kept quiet in Tobias, not when it has to do with the Corbetts."

He sat in the old wicker chair. It creaked under his weight.

"So what's new?" A bleakness showed beneath his cocky grin.

"And," she continued relentlessly, "many will assume you left town eight years ago because you knew you'd gotten Lily pregnant."

His grin hardened into a grimace and the bleakness spread. But only for a moment, and then he hid it. Completely and coldly.

"What about you, Fran? Do you think I left town because I knew Lily was pregnant?"

"No."

His blue eyes examined her. "What about before I came back? Did you think it before you witnessed me being pole-axed by Nell?"

"No," she said. "I never thought you left because Lily was pregnant."

His grin resurfaced. "Ah, but then, you always had a crush on me."

"No." She gave that all the firmness it deserved. "I never had a crush on you. I thought you were a jerk. Possibly re-deemable, but definitely a jerk."

He laughed, and this time it was the throw-back-his-head-and-let-it-all-out laugh she remembered from a young Zach. The older he'd grown, the less she'd heard it.

She was glad he'd recaptured it in the west or Virginia or wherever he'd been.

Fran awakened early.

Earlier than she had to. Was there anything worse?

Yes, waking with Zach Corbett's voice repeating a trio of sentences over and over in her head.

Led astray by an older man, huh? Bet that never happened to you again. So you should thank me.

She could get a few more minutes of sleep. But that would delay her making phone calls to the tree mover, to nurseries to check shipments, to the seed supplier about packets to be given away at the opening. Delaying the phone calls would delay getting to Bliss House. She should get up.

God, she hated getting up in the morning. It was so com-fortable and cozy in her bed....

Except for when she had a voice dunning in her head.

Led astray by an older man, huh? Bet that never happened to you again. You should thank me.

That's why she'd awakened so darn early this morning, because of this sense of another presence in the house—Zach Corbett, of all the people in the world—and because of the knowledge that she held full responsibility for putting him here.

Taking on one more thing, Rob would say with that concerned look.

And her brother was right. He was even right about what he hadn't said, at least not yet—that all these things were tying her to Tobias, to this house and to this life alone.

She knew he felt guilty that she'd been the one to come home to be with their dying father. That's why he kept saying the house was hers alone, even though the will clearly left it to both of them.

What he didn't understand was the reward. Yes, she'd missed some things left behind when she'd moved back to Tobias from Madison. But she couldn't have been anywhere else that last year of Daddy's life.

And, yes, maybe she had gotten tied into Tobias's daily life. But, really, Rob didn't need to worry about her. She *could* say no. She just seldom wanted to. When the gardens were done, though, she would seriously look at her life and what to do with it.

She rolled over, gazing out the back window that faced Steve and Annette's house.

She wondered how they were doing this morning. And Nell?

She sniffed, dreaming of coffee. Then she flopped onto her back. Coffee had to be made, not dreamed.

After Annette became involved with Steve again this spring, she'd asked Fran flat out if Nell was at her house too much. Fran had assured her that she loved having Nell around. She'd looked after Nell during their honeymoon.

She sat up in bed. That *was* coffee she smelled.

She swung her legs over the side of the bed. The day would be warm, but the room still held the night's chill. She slid her feet into her slippers and pulled on her robe.

Fran had great faith in Nell, and especially in the family Steve, Annette and Nell had become. But Nell was not yet eight. And it had been a jolt when Steve had told her earlier this year that he was not her biological father. A jolt she hadn't fully absorbed before she was hit with the new one of her biological father showing up.

Fran looked back at her cozy bed, where she could sleep without thinking about any of this, before closing the door.

She headed down the stairs to face the man who'd brewed the delicious-smelling coffee and who had said: *Led astray by an older man, huh? Bet that never happened to you again. You should thank me.*

But he couldn't see into her head to know the response that had formed before she was awake enough to stop it this morning: *No, it wasn't an older man who led me astray. It was one my age who made a fool of me. And it will never happen again.*

First thing Zach knew of Fran's presence was when he turned from the sink, where he'd been making orange juice, to grab the phone before it rang a second time and found it already in her hand.

She listened a moment, staring into space.

"No comment," she said, firm and unemotional.

He heard a voice still coming through the receiver as she hung up. She shuffled toward the coffeemaker.

"What was that about, Fran?"

"Some business of Rob's."

She poured herself a cup of coffee, clearly having no intention of telling him more.

He'd awakened well before dawn, knowing sleep wouldn't return. Sometimes that happened when his body was still on a different time zone or a different shift. That wasn't the reason this time.

He'd pulled on sweats, slipped out of the house and run through dark streets. Just like he used to.

Despite the changes in town, he'd found his way off the height where Corbett House sat. The only other spot close to being that high was the hilltop that held Bliss House.

At the lakeside he'd turned and looked up at the two darkened lumps that were all he could see of Corbett House and Bliss House, the two very different houses built by descendants of the town's founder, Tobias Corbett. He'd always considered it an accident of birth that he hadn't been born to the eccentric side of the family. He'd have fit in over there at Bliss House.

*Accident of birth…*like Nell?

Zach tried to shut his mind down from thoughts of what had brought him back to Tobias and what he'd found here.

He pushed his body to make the full circuit around the lake, knowing it wasn't the safest thing to run in the dark. But he'd done it before, and he'd survived. And there wasn't much more traffic than there'd been nine years ago. He scared the hell out of a deer and got a shock himself at the sight of the old resort on the far side of the lake, spruced up and its parking lot full.

He'd pounded back up Corbett Hill with glimpses of newspaper-delivery trucks poking along the side streets and a stray light or two pinpointing early risers.

For half a second after he rounded the corner onto Kelly Street muscle memory almost led him to the back entry of Corbett House.

Instead, he slowed, looking diagonally across the street to the house Steve lived in with his wife and daughter.

Chester gave a warning growl when Zach entered the porch. He talked, letting her remember that Fran had said he was okay.

His shower was hot and long, but not long enough.

With more dark to get through without letting the thoughts free, he'd headed to the kitchen, fixing coffee, checking supplies.

As she watched him now, Fran showed no sign of recognizing that the coffee had been brewed for some time or that he had a list going on the counter.

After his shower, he'd put on a T-shirt and workout shorts as a nod to modesty. But to meet her standards he should have worn a three-piece suit.

Her robe covered her from neck to the slippers that revealed only the tips of her toes. Not only covered her, but provided a double layer down the front, where the robe overlapped because it was too big for her.

Like the clothes she'd had on yesterday—way too big for her, verging on the sloppy oversize style some teenagers affected. Somehow he didn't think Fran suffered from a slavish devotion to fashion trends, however. Besides, the knot where the robe's tie cinched her waist spoke more of security than fashion.

No way did she recognize that pulling the tie so tight only emphasized her waist, as well as the intriguing curves above and below it, curves hidden by those drapes of clothing she'd worn yesterday…except for when a cooperative breeze came along.

"What are you smiling at?" she demanded over her coffee cup.

"Still not a morning person, huh, Fran?"

"What makes you think I'm not a morning person?"

"Memory. I spent enough mornings in this kitchen to know."

She scowled. "I don't remember you here in the mornings."

He laughed. "That's because you were asleep—which was my point. You'd sleep until the last possible moment to still get to school on time. Your mom used to fret about you not getting breakfast."

Her brief huff acknowledged the truth of his memory. "Scrambled eggs okay?"

"Great. But you don't have to—"

"I'm cooking for myself, might as well make you some, too." She turned on the burner, retrieved a pan, the eggs and seasonings, sprayed the pan with olive oil and cracked eggs into a bowl with the mindless ease of routine.

When the phone rang again he made one move toward it, but she said quickly, "I'll get it."

Her caution eased with the first word she heard, and he relaxed, too. It wasn't the same caller. But he didn't stop watching her.

"Tell her Chester and the puppies are great…. Of course. You don't have to ask—this is your home…. Yes, of course Kay can stay on if that's what you think is best. Now or whenever…."

She gave a slight smile—less with her mouth than with a shifting at the corners of her eyes.

"No, Rob, that won't bother me. But maybe not your old room. You'll want more space and, uh…" She glanced toward Zach but her gaze bounced away before connecting. "Someone else is staying here for a while, so your room might not be the best…. We can talk about it later…. No…. Yes…. Rob— Don't be ridiculous, Rob. It's Zach. Zach Corbett....Very much so.... That's why he's staying here.... It's going to take time.... I don't know."

While she said farewells, Zach opened a drawer and found place mats and napkins where they used to be kept.

"That was Rob," she said.

"Figured that out."

"He and his fiancée, Kay, are coming for the weekend."

"If I'm going to be in the way—"

"No. There's plenty of room."

He nodded. "It'll be good to see Rob."

She stepped aside as he zeroed in on the silverware drawer.

"What were you doing in our kitchen as a kid while I was sleeping in?" she asked his back as he set places in front of stools at the counter.

"Talking. Having some breakfast."

"Why?" she asked bluntly. "You always had great cooks at Corbett House."

"Never liked cold breakfasts," he murmured, facing her. Her lips parted to dispute that Lana Corbett's cooks had served cold meals, then he saw the understanding in her eyes that he wasn't talking about food, and her frown cleared. He kept talking then so she couldn't serve up any sympathy, a dish he'd never cared for, hot or cold. "I started tagging along with Steve when he came to meet Rob to walk to school when they were in grade school. I kept coming until…"

She turned her back to him, removing the eggs from the pan with a spatula, but her voice was steady. "Until my mom got sick."

"Yeah."

"That's something Nell and I have talked about." She poured juice, put the glasses on the end of the counter for him to retrieve. "Something we have in common."

He wouldn't have introduced the topic, but she was probing, and he wouldn't step back from it, either. Not entirely, anyway.

"But you still had a dad."

"So does Nell. And now she has Annette, too."

"You're saying I should disappear? Butt out of the girl's life?"

"No." She placed a plate of eggs in front of him. "Not without some resolution. That would be the worst possible thing for Nell."

She topped off their coffee mugs, then sat.

"So I'm supposed to sit here and wait for her to work out if she wants to see me?"

She paused with a forkful of fluffy eggs on its way to her mouth. Then she nodded. As calm as ever. "Yes, you are. Also talk to Steve and Annette about the situation." She chewed the eggs thoughtfully before adding with a glint in her eyes, "And bust your butt working on the Bliss House gardens."

"Great, just great." Sarcasm snapped the words, but for some reason he felt a tug of a grin as he dove into the eggs.

Both plates were nearly empty when she spoke again.

"You might also consider mending fences with your mother."

"When hell freezes over."

Chapter Four

From her command post at the table, with most of today's calls checked off and her stomach reminding her it was past lunchtime, Fran looked out the window, waiting on hold yet again.

She'd told Zach that she needed to make phone calls this morning, leaving him free. He had left before she came downstairs from getting dressed and returned a short while ago with a different car.

She'd been on hold then, too.

"Turned in the rental, got this one used," he'd said when he'd come in and placed a key on the counter before getting a drink of water. "Here's a spare key in case you need it."

"You bought a car?"

"More economical than renting one for any length of time. You were the one who said I might be here awhile."

Just then the phone line clicked and a voice spoke. Zach waved his understanding of the situation and went back outside.

But she was far from understanding Zach.

Even as she'd confirmed the arrival date of the main order of tulip bulbs, questions had piled up in her head.

Who would have believed somebody would just go out and buy a car? Especially somebody who hadn't even been sure that he would knock on his mother's door yesterday. And yet that didn't surprise her half as much as what Zach Corbett had bought. A sedan with a reputation for reliability and not a single pretension to hotness. He must not have much money or he'd never own something like that.

She'd completed the tulip call and dialed again. She'd tried for more than a week to reach the man who'd promised to move the donated trees. This time, at least, she got as far as having someone tell her to hold for him. It was sad when being put on hold was a sign of progress.

She looked out the window now and was caught short once again by the sight of the car Zach had bought.

Even with no money to burn, surely he'd had a choice of color, and this was not what she would have expected. The car was red—technically. But it was a deep, mellow maroon, not fiery salsa.

For some reason that reminded her of the phone conversation with her brother earlier today.

She'd fended off Rob's questions about who was staying at the house until he'd started down the absurd track of it being someone of romantic interest to her. She'd stopped that by telling him it was Zach.

My God, he's alive?

Very much so.

Good Lord, what about Nell?

That's why he's staying here.

*Lana wouldn't—? No, of course she wouldn't. God—
Steve's got to be going nuts—after all these years of being
afraid Zach was dead. But Nell... How the hell are they going
to work this out?*

It's going to take time.

If Zach relinquishes any claim to Nell.... Will he?

I don't know.

Where the hell has he been? What's he been doing?

That one had stopped her.

She'd been spared answering, though, because Rob had realized the time and had to go. He hadn't even given her his
usual big-brotherly be-careful line.

Maybe that was because he knew Zach Corbett was no danger to her—not to her virtue and not to her heart. The latter
because she'd never fallen for the Tobias heartthrob as a kid,
so why should she at this point? The former because Zach had
liked girls who were as loud and brash and showy as that motorcycle of his.

Her gaze still on the sedate sedan, Fran shifted in her chair.

Steve came out of his garage, glanced toward his brother,
then began digging in the flower bed alongside the driveway.
It wasn't unheard of for Steve to come home for lunch, but it
was strange to see him digging in the garden wearing work
clothes. Annette's car was there and so was Nell's bike, so the
whole family had had lunch together.

Zach took two large bags emblazoned with a discount
store's logo out of the sedan's trunk, setting them aside. Next
he took out a smaller bag and began stowing things from it
around the driver's seat.

That roused her curiosity. When he moved to the passenger side, he leaned in the open door, apparently working at

something on the hump between the front seats—and giving her a fine view of worn jeans stretched over a rear end that roused…well, yes, curiosity, but also other responses.

Fran jerked her gaze away. Nell emerged from the garage on her bike, her school books in the basket. Fran couldn't hear the words, but she'd heard Steve's usual message to Nell many times—reminding her to be careful, to work hard, and wishing her a good afternoon at school.

Steve watched Nell, but from his angle he wouldn't be able to see the way her gaze zoomed to Zach, still leaning inside the car.

Steve watched his daughter out of sight, then turned and looked at Zach. Zach, straightening out of the passenger door, looked back. Fran suspected he'd been watching Nell's departure through the car windows.

Steve dropped the shovel, pivoted and went inside, leaving the garage door open.

Zach stood with his hands on his narrow hips, staring at his brother's house. He dropped his head a moment, then straightened and strode across the street.

Fran let out a breath she hadn't known she'd been holding.

But the air she pulled in to replace it didn't bring any satisfaction. What was happening between the brothers? Would Zach get his answers? At least the ones Steve could provide. Did Zach have any inkling that most of his answers could only come from inside him?

Would Zach and Steve be able to resurrect the connection they'd once had? As different as they had always been, everyone with eyes knew the Corbett brothers were bound by loyalty, pride and, yes, love. But had Zach broken those ties when he'd left, not letting Steve even know he was alive?

Fran tried not to imagine what they were saying, tried not to worry how relationships and lives might be changing.

"Hello, Ms. Dalton?" The voice in her ear made her jump, and she almost lost the phone.

"Yes. Yes, Mr. Buchell. I'm calling to confirm the schedule we talked about."

And then Fran saw Lana Corbett walking across the street toward Steve's house—a house she had never been inside to Fran's knowledge—and for Fran there was no question of *not* worrying.

Steve opened the back door before Zach could knock. Without a word he stepped back, clearing the way.

As Zach walked past his older brother he caught a motion from the corner of his eye. He turned and found Steve eyeing him, specifically the top of his head.

Steve used to have more than an inch of height on him. Now Zach had the advantage.

"I grew after I left," he said. In more ways than one.

"Did you?"

The skeptical edge to that comment would have cut through the minimal control the younger Zach had had over his temper, and Steve knew it. The younger Steve wouldn't have wielded that sort of edge.

If Zach hadn't gotten the message already it was clear now—Steve would use any weapon if he felt it necessary in any matter concerning Nell.

But Zach's control wasn't held by a thread anymore.

"Would you like something to drink, Zach?" Annette stood on the far side of the counter that separated the entryway from the working area of the kitchen.

"No—" His scan of the room stopped on three wipe-off

calendars labeled This Month, Next Month and The Month After. Underneath the headings were a dizzying array of multicolored appointments, deadlines and reminders. The life of a family. He forced himself to add, "Thank you."

"I hear you think you're going to stay in Tobias and work on the gardens." Steve moved around him and stood beside Annette, his hands jammed in the pockets of his slacks.

Steve wore a white dress shirt, a subtle blue tie and quality leather shoes. He looked like what he was, a contented, prosperous, hardworking official. Zach wore jeans, a black T-shirt and running shoes. So he looked like what he was, too.

"I *am* staying and helping out Fran at Bliss House while this gets sorted out. As I'm sure Fran told you."

"There's nothing to sort—"

Annette talked over her husband. "Zach, you must have forgotten how Tobias operates if you think we didn't hear about your plans from a dozen sources by now. And none of them was Fran."

"You can't just come back here and pick up like you never left," Steve said, calmer now.

Zach pulled out a stool from under the counter and sat. As a symbol that he wasn't going anywhere just yet it was obvious, but he also needed to sit because his muscles suddenly wanted to jump and twitch. His legs hadn't felt like that since… No, damn it, he was not going to think about that now.

"I thought you wanted me back," he said. "Fran said you'd put ads in papers looking for me."

"Yes, I did. And you never responded. Did you see them?"

"I saw…a few. I wasn't ready to come back."

Steve's face twisted. Zach didn't know if it was from anger or pain or both. Annette slipped her hand around his arm, slid it down to where his hand disappeared into his slacks pocket.

"I had private detectives looking for you," Steve said.

"*You* did. I thought…" He'd thought the ads and detectives were Lana's efforts to reel in the wayward Corbett. "Well, I wouldn't recommend you hire either of them again. The guy from Milwaukee stuck strictly to the paper trail and it wasn't hard to throw him off. The one from Beloit was better. But he tipped his hand, so when he showed up I already had a buddy who looks nothing like me ready to stand in for me. Only took a couple of days to persuade the guy he'd followed a false trail."

"We thought you could be dead and you thought it was a game?" Steve demanded, his anger clear.

"No. I knew it was my life." For a single beat of his pulse Zach saw an understanding in Steve's eyes, then it was gone. "I can't say it would have made a difference if I'd known it was you looking for me. I couldn't have come back then."

"But now you can?" Steve looked at him with the penetrating stare Zach used to think could see his every thought.

"Yeah, now I can," he said. Though it wasn't the truth. He hadn't had a choice. "Steve, tell me what happened. We don't have to solve everything now, but why did—"

The back door opened and Lana Corbett stalked in.

"Mother?" Steve and Annette stared at her as if she might be an apparition.

"You are discussing the future of the Corbetts. You cannot shut me out of that. You must have DNA tests."

The clipped pronouncements and the focus on the vaunted name *Corbett* were exactly how Zach remembered his mother. A string of responses rose up. But her last edict blocked them all in his throat.

"Lily lied from beginning to end," Lana continued, "so we have no assurance that she didn't lie about Nell's father, as well. Why you insisted on accepting her word for everything, Steven, I never will understand. Only through a DNA test will we know for certain. As I told you at the start, there is every possibility that Zachary is not the father, so—"

"She's mine."

Two words. They could change a life. Zach hadn't known he was going to speak them. He'd thought he'd broken that habit years ago. But here he was, back in Tobias, facing his mother, and words were coming out before he considered them.

At least these had been the right words.

"Nell is my daughter." Zach said it again.

"You can't possibly know—"

He met Lana's cold certainty with deeper certainty. "I know. Lily wasn't sleeping with anyone else."

She'd wanted to land a Corbett from the time she was a high-school junior angling for Steve. Steve had broken it off before he left for college and then he started dating Annette. Zach knew damn well Lily had come on to him in hopes of making Steve jealous and winning him back from Annette.

It was when Zach had realized that Lily had given up on that hope and turned her attention to securing him—second-best Corbett, but still a Corbett—that he'd broken up with her. When she was using him, that was one thing. But to let her think he'd marry her…no.

But even when he'd been as blunt as he could be, she hadn't given up hope. She certainly wouldn't have jeopardized her ambitions to become the next Lana Corbett by having sex with anyone else.

"Besides," Zach drawled, "take another look at the family album, Lana. The pictures of Father as a boy. He and Nell could be twins."

The phone rang. It seemed to come from a distance,

though Zach knew it was right here in the kitchen. Annette answered it.

"It wouldn't matter if Nell didn't have a drop of Corbett blood, Mother. She's *my* daughter, and nothing—" Steve gave Zach a long look "—is going to change that."

Lana pursed her mouth. "My point is—"

Annette's urgent voice cut across her mother-in-law's. Zach saw she'd already hung up. "Steve, Zach, Nell's on her way back. She must have forgotten something. Unless…"

A look passed between Annette and Steve that piled layers on layers. The only one Zach caught was concern.

"She'll come in the back. Go out the front, Zach," Steve ordered.

"I won't creep out like some—"

"The hell you won't. This is my house and if I have to—"

"Stop it!" Annette's demand silenced them both. Zach was aware that she looked from her husband to him and back, but most of his attention was focused straight ahead—meeting Steve's glare. "Nell is the one who's important. And she will *not* walk into this house to find you two arguing."

Steve broke the look, turning to Annette.

"I'll go," Zach said. "For now. But I'm not going away. I—"

"If that's a threat—"

"Steve," Annette warned.

"I'm not threatening," Zach said. "I'm making a promise. I'm not going anywhere until…until I know."

"Know what?" Lana demanded.

"Know what I need to know."

Zach found Fran standing beside the overloaded table writing a note, which she slid into the thickest folder.

"So what's the plan?"

She looked up at his abrupt entry and equally abrupt question.

"I'm happy to tell you the plan for the garden, but that isn't the plan you should be thinking about now."

Her tone added meaning to the words. Fran must have seen him scuttle out the front door of Steve's house as Nell went in the back. He'd heard their questions and answers— why wasn't she at school, a forgotten paper—and then he'd quick-timed it across the street to Fran's house like some fleeing felon.

"What's the plan at the gardens today?" He met Fran's gaze.

"Zach—"

"The gardens."

She sighed.

"We'll be working the soil in the section of the Grandmother's Garden where the Garden Club ladies will be planting tomorrow." Her tone changed at the end, and he knew she was watching Steve back his SUV out of his driveway with Nell in the passenger seat. Presumably heading off to take the girl to school. Probably also to ensure she had no contact with Zach. "Zach, you have to be—"

"Patient. I know. Ready to go?"

She nodded, picked up her purse, then opened her mouth again. Before she could say anything, he held the door for her to go out, then got his question in.

"What are the Garden Club ladies going to plant?"

"Tomorrow will be mostly tiger lilies for next year and pansies to add color for the opening. When the bulbs arrive, they'll put in the daffodils and hyacinths—but only after a snowball, a white lilac and another peony are in place. Plus the tulips in several areas. Next spring, the Grandmother's

Garden will get a shot of color with phlox, Canterbury bells, sweet William, cottage pinks, rose campion—that's a lychnis." She caught herself. "But you're not interested in that. The important thing is the soil needs to be worked in those areas. And carefully, to avoid disturbing existing plants."

He'd known that question was the way to get her off the topic of his family. Her enthusiasm even eased some of the sourness in his mood.

"What's your idea of working the soil?"

"Dig at least a foot, break it up, add plenty of humus. If there's time before dark I'd love to work the soil for the kitchen garden, too. We can add humus, mulch and let that work in over the winter. Perhaps set up fences for the vining vegetables... Well, we'll see about that."

"What kind of vegetables are you planning?"

"Asparagus, pepper, lettuce, salsify—the Victorians loved that, called it the oyster plant—beans, beets, carrots, onions, cucumber, tomato, cabbage. Lots of herbs." She was so lost in delight she hardly seemed to notice he'd steered her to her car. "Oh, and rhubarb. Muriel Henderson—she's in the Garden Club and is one of the craftspeople—has a great rhubarb crumble recipe we can serve in the tearoom."

He opened the driver's door before circling to the passenger side.

"And we'll have flowers from the cutting garden—a border all around the kitchen garden."

"Why not cut flowers from the other gardens?"

"Because that would deplete them."

"Hard to believe a chain saw could deplete them the way you're going," he said over the top of her car.

She clicked her tongue, but her eyes creased. She started to get in.

"Fran." She straightened, looking at him over the top of the car. "We didn't settle a damned thing."

Fran craned her neck to examine a trio of peonies near the construction.

"Still there, Fran. Just like I promised. Though I won't take the rap if that cat of Miss Trudi's has done something to them."

She jumped at the amused voice behind her. She turned to Max Trevetti, Annette's older brother and the man behind the renovations of Bliss House. Walking with him toward the southwest corner of the house where she and Zach stood were Suz Grant and Miss Trudi. Fran had been showing Zach what needed to be done before they went to the shed for tools.

"Max, I wasn't…" Fran gave up the protest, because she *had* been checking up. "Thank you for taking care of them. Max, I don't know if you remember Zach—Zach Corbett, Steve's brother. He's going to help me with the gardens for, uh, now."

"Zach," Max said neutrally. From his expression he already knew about Zach's arrival and his relationship to Nell. Max had practically raised Annette, and he was fond of Nell and Steve. So maybe neutral was the best anyone could hope for in his dealings with Zach. "Don't know that we've ever been introduced officially."

"I remember you." Zach made a motion as if to extend his hand then thought better of it.

"Indeed, you are related by marriage now that Steve and Annette are husband and wife," Miss Trudi said.

Tension rose as if someone had turned the knob on a gas burner, sending the flames higher. Miss Trudi smiled benignly at all of them as if she didn't have a clue her hand had been the one twisting that knob.

Fran introduced Zach to Suz, then quickly added, "Max's

company has done all the work here. Max and Suz's company, I should say, now that she's a partner." Fran had found exactly the right antidote to ease Max's tension—mention Suz Grant's name and the man practically melted.

"Looks like great work." Zach scanned Bliss House's facade.

"Trevetti Building always does good work. But this has been some project. Everybody's working flat out. Including this one." Max tipped his head toward Fran. "She's been working on those gardens hard enough to put my two best men combined to shame."

"Your men have been great. And with the Garden Club—"

"Nice ladies," Max said. "Not quite the muscle to lean into a shovel as Zach here."

A voice from inside called Max and Suz. They nodded and went into the house.

Miss Trudi smiled at Zach. "Have you talked to your mother?"

Fran wanted to close her eyes, tap her heels together three times and return those words to Miss Trudi's mouth.

In fairness, Miss Trudi didn't know Zach had gone to talk to Steve and Annette today, didn't know Lana had entered into the discussion, too, somehow, and didn't know that Zach had emerged with his blue eyes suddenly haggard, even as he'd stiffly kept her at a distance—until that one short sentence before he got in the car.

We didn't settle a damned thing.

How did she know it was a concession for him to tell her even that?

"Why should I talk to Lana?" Zach's low tone should have been a warning.

Miss Trudi tipped her head, studying him. "At what point did you begin to refer to your mother as Lana?"

"When I lived under her roof. Better to use her name than a description, don't you think?"

"What I think is—"

"Sorry, Miss Trudi," Fran interrupted. "We'd love to chat, but with the work I have lined up for Zach, we need to get busy. I'm sure you understand. It's for the good of Bliss House." Miss Trudi turned to study her now, but Fran wasn't waiting around for a report card. "C'mon, Zach. Let's get the supplies."

She started off, sensing Zach at her right shoulder.

"Oh, yes, Fran, dear," Miss Trudi's voice came from behind them, "I do understand."

"You go ahead and get a shower first," Fran told him as they crossed the darkened back porch. "That hot water heater isn't up to two showers at the same time. I'll start dinner."

But first she greeted the dog, let it out, gave it food and water, and checked each puppy.

As if she hadn't worked hard enough as it was today, Zach thought sourly. She had matched him nearly shovelful for shovelful. They'd finished what she'd called the Grandmother's Garden, but had barely broken ground on the kitchen garden, which as far as he could see had produced only weeds for decades.

"Let's get takeout."

She looked over her shoulder from where she sat on the porch floor brushing Chester. "If you want. Pizza or Chinese?"

"Your choice, my treat."

"You're working for your board as well as the bed, Zach, so—"

"I told you I'd take care of that myself. Tomorrow I'll get groceries. You don't have much."

"I do, too. There's plenty—"

"Just place the order so it'll be ready when you are."

He walked inside. He heard her mutter something, apparently to the dog, about arrogant males.

When he came downstairs she was on the phone in the kitchen.

She must have taken a shower while he'd called work, because the smudges were gone from her face and neck and she wore clean sweats.

Was this another call like the one that had drawn her stiff "No comment" this morning? He could say a few choice things to anyone who made Fran react like that.

But Zach knew this call was different when Fran looked over her shoulder at him and said, "Yes, he is."

She made no move to give him the receiver. After a few innocuous phrases she hung up and said, "Steve's on his way over. I'll go upstairs so you can talk here."

She picked up two folders then flipped through a stack in apparent pursuit of more material.

"No. You stay here. We can talk on the porch."

"It's getting cool."

"Maybe that's good." He gave her a dry grin.

"You're family. You love each other. You'll work it out."

"More family than I expected when I came back."

"Surely it occurred to you Steve might have children by now?"

"If it did, it never occurred to me that he'd have my kid."

Her lips parted, then closed on a firm line, holding in captivity the words he saw brewing in her eyes.

"I know, I know," he said to the message he saw there. "But…"

She glanced out the window that had a view of the steps. "He's here."

Zach came out of the house at the same time Steve stepped into the porch.

"Shall we sit." Steve made it neither invitation nor question. Zach had dealt with enough people accustomed to leading to know it was the voice of a man who expected what he said to happen.

In that way, his brother was exactly the man Zach had expected him to become.

They took seats in chairs at right angles and divided by a corner table. Zach noticed Steve looked older than he had yesterday in Corbett House's entry hall. Did his own face have fresh lines and new grooves?

"Seems like the last time we had an important talk it was on a porch, too," he said.

His position in the Corbett family was like a building that had come crashing down and the issue now was finding out if anything buried under the rubble had survived. Only a fool tried to yank from the bottom layers first. You had to de-layer, one level at a time, checking where you were after each one. That was the only way to get to what might be trapped underneath.

Steve inclined his head. "When you told me to get out—"

"To get away."

"—and leave Tobias and the Corbett name behind. You gave no indication you intended to do that. But even if you had, I couldn't do it. Even though I'm not really a Corbett."

Zach released a breath through his teeth. So Steve knew that Lana had been pregnant by another man when she married Ambrose Corbett.

"I wanted to tell you," Zach said.

"How did you know?"

"Bits and pieces over the years. Things Lana said to me that she never said to you. And then when she had to accept that you were going to marry Annette, that you had a different future in mind than she'd planned, she said…more. Enough that it couldn't be explained away, couldn't be anything else. How long have you known?"

"That summer after you left," Steve said. "You'd given me a shove in that direction, and after it was clear you weren't coming back anytime soon—another important *talk* on a porch—"

He meant Zach's final, shouting declaration to Lana more than eight years ago that he was getting out. Zach didn't remember much of it. Just flashes. The scent of lilacs from the bush by the corner of the porch. A freeze-frame view of Steve and Annette side by side in the swing at the far end. The angry tap-tap of his mother's heels as she came after him, adamant that he would live the life she wanted him to live. Finally, the burst of power under him as he got on the bike, the defiance of the tires gashing the lawn as he rode across it, and then only sound and motion, blotting out everything else.

"—and I followed the trail," Steve concluded. "Got confirmation."

"At least you got Lana to face reality."

"Confirmation didn't come from Mother. She didn't know that I knew until this past spring when…I made some changes."

"You were more his son than I was."

Ambrose Corbett, who had married beautiful Lana when he was more than fifty and she barely twenty, was a nebulous presence in Zach's memory. A vaguely benign but distant figure. It was mostly in retrospect, after Ambrose died and Lana was free to enforce her ideas of what a Corbett should be, that he'd realized how benign.

"He loved us both," Steve said.

"More than you can say for Lana." Zach was certain the words held no heat but only a recognition of the reality of their mother.

"I'm not sure that's fair to Mother," his older brother said. "She's not an easy woman, but Annette's helped me see these past months that maybe Mother can change. And she's been better—more open."

They were talking around the core issue, circling it.

But that was okay with Zach.

"Annette must be a damned saint to see good in Lana, especially considering the way she fought you two getting married, and when she couldn't win that one, taking over your wedding."

"Not our second wedding," Steve said with a small smile.

"Second wedding?"

"Fran didn't tell you?"

"Fran seems to feel I should get my information from you."

Steve didn't respond to that. At least not directly. "Annette and I didn't get married eight years ago. We did get married in June."

Zach knew this feeling. It was what happened when you arrived on site after an earthquake. As you took in the devastation and tried to imagine what it had felt like for the people who'd lived through it—or those who hadn't. You felt the earth give and shake with an aftershock, and you knew it was only a tiny echo of the main event, but it didn't make the ground feel any more solid under your feet.

"Why? You called off your wedding with Annette? But—"

"No, we didn't call it off. But Lily..." Steve drove his hands through his hair. "Lily came to me after you left. First she wanted to know when you'd be back. When she realized

I didn't know where you were any more than anyone else, she said she was pregnant with your baby. It fit. I'd seen you together, and you'd said—"

"I remember."

Steve had waited up for him that night in early spring, opening the door to his room when Zach would have passed by. Zach hadn't waited for him to speak.

I thought I recognized your car passing the motel. So what are you going to do? Tell me the facts of life?

Steve had looked pained. But all he'd said was, *Be careful.*

Zach didn't remember everything he'd said. Something about it being too late for the warning. And he'd told Steve he knew Lily had gone after him only because she'd hoped to make Steve jealous. But he remembered his final words.

Oh, I know, Saint Steven would have resisted temptation. But nobody's ever accused me of being a saint. There are benefits to being the fallen Corbett. Definite benefits.

After he'd left he'd thought about those words. Thought about how he'd pursued the benefits of being the fallen Corbett. Thought about how he'd taunted his brother with that Saint Steven title.

"I said I'd make sure she and the baby were taken care of," Steve said, "but…I guess she had doubts. Wanted a sure thing. Lily burst into our wedding and said Annette and I couldn't get married because she was carrying my child."

"Your—?! Christ! She always wanted to snag you, be Mrs. Steven Corbett. But Annette must have known…"

He didn't bother to finish as Steve shook his head.

"There were problems between us. And that—that was like the tap of the hammer hitting the flaw just right so the diamond shatters." The lines on his older brother's face eased, then reformed into a smile. "At least that's what I thought, what both of us thought, until Annette came back to Tobias last March. First time we'd talked since the wedding."

"You patched it up?"

Steve shook his head. "We made something better."

"I'm glad, Steve," he said.

"Thank you."

But that simple moment couldn't withstand the flood of complicated emotions dividing them.

Steve sat back, straight and in charge.

"After things fell apart with Annette, the fiasco at the wedding, Lily said if I didn't marry her, she'd make sure no Corbett ever saw the baby. So I married her."

Zach felt curses rise in his throat, along with bile. "You let her blackmail you into marrying her?"

"It didn't much matter to me at that point, not with Annette gone. And there was the baby. Being married gave me legal rights. It was the right decision. Lily hardly even looked at Nell. A few months after Nell was born, Lily left. The divorce was generous enough that she was happy to sign, so it was quick and painless. Nell wasn't quite two when Lily died in a car accident. She was high."

Zach tried to absorb this. Steve had married a woman he didn't love, had cared for an infant on his own, had taken on single parenthood. "Why, Steve? Why did you do it?"

"Because through Annette I know what it means not to have a father. Because Ambrose Corbett was a father to me when I didn't have one. Because the baby was yours. But you've got to understand, we're a family—Annette, Nell and me. We're the family Nell knows, the family she loves."

"She's never had a chance to love me."

"Whose fault is that?"

"How could I have known?"

"Would it have mattered?"

Before Zach could recover from that blow, Steve continued. "You're my brother. Nothing will ever change that. But I won't let you hurt Nell."

"I'm going to know her, Steve."

"That's up to her. As my brother, as her uncle—I would never deny you that…if she wants it. But I'm her father, Zach. I have been for almost eight years and I always will be."

What does that make me?

Zach didn't say the words—maybe he didn't want to hear the answer.

Steve continued immediately. "Annette and I decided. If there's going to be any contact, it'll be because Nell initiates it. You don't go to her. If Nell wants to see you, okay. But not alone. You only see her if I'm there or Annette or Fran or Miss Trudi, someone Nell knows and trusts completely."

"God, Steve—you think I'd snatch her? You think I'd terrorize a kid?"

"We don't know, Zach. We don't know you."

Chapter Five

Fran emptied leftovers from the last cardboard box of Chinese food into a plastic container. Ordinarily, she would have taken the containers right to the fridge. But with Zach pacing erratically, she opted to stay put.

He'd been silent while they ate in front of the TV. In fact, she couldn't remember him even looking at the screen except for a short report about a building bombed in Malaysia. He showed no interest in the sitcom that followed the news.

As soon as she stood to clear their empty dishes from the coffee table, he rose and helped her. Then it was as if moving had released something in him, as if he couldn't stop moving.

Zach Corbett prowling her kitchen shrank the space to an eighth of its size.

She put the last utensil in the dishwasher, gave the sink a final wipe, then turned and leaned back against it.

"Do you want to talk? Or would you rather I leave it alone?"

"The hell if I know," he said, not breaking stride. He pivoted and started back. "A daughter. My God, I've got a daughter, Fran."

"Not what you expected when you came back, I know."

"It wasn't like I expected everything to hold still while I was gone, but..." He pushed his hands through his hair. "I thought everyone would be okay—better—without me here. Steve, especially. Instead, my leaving screwed up his wedding to Annette, and he got tangled up with Lily and then raised a baby—my baby—alone. Christ."

"You didn't screw up his wedding to Annette. Lily did that. Don't try to take on responsibility for everything, only what you're responsible for. And, actually, it wasn't just Lily. Your mother contributed, and Steve and Annette ultimately were responsible for how they reacted."

"Lana? What did she have to do with it?"

"Apparently she told Lily right before the wedding that Lily wouldn't get a cent of Corbett money. That contradicted Steve's promises. Lily was afraid she'd be left on her own, so she interrupted the wedding and declared the baby was Steve's. She told Steve later that she'd expected him to deny it by saying the baby was actually yours—that's what she wanted, a public statement that the Corbetts had a responsibility to her. When Annette walked out, Lily saw a better opportunity, and she went for it. She pressured Steve to give her and the baby the Corbett name. I wasn't aware of all this then, but even I could see that Steve was in no shape to resist Lily. It was like he'd come unplugged from the universe."

"God, and all this is supposed to make me feel less like I screwed up my brother's life?"

"Steve would be the first one to tell you Nell has *made* his life, not screwed it up."

"I'll never know, because Steve has a wall up." He waved that off, as if he hadn't meant to say it. Too late. She'd heard the hurt. "None of that makes me less responsible for what happened."

"As I said, they're responsible for how they reacted to what happened. And when Nell was born…well, Steve plugged back in. Besides, Annette says they wouldn't have lasted together then. They needed the years apart to become the people they are now, adults who totally love each other…and who totally love Nell."

"And who totally want me to disappear."

"That's the worst thing you could do now."

He gave her a narrow-eyed look that nearly hid the blue but at the same time concentrated the intensity.

"So you don't think I should slink away and leave the happy little family alone, too."

"No. And I don't believe Steve or Annette think that, either. Most of all I don't believe it would be good for Nell."

He stopped pacing and faced her. "How is my sticking around better for her than my taking off?"

"She has a lot of questions, a lot of doubts. If you went away—again—before they were answered, they could haunt her forever. You came back, and now you have a responsibility to stay and see this through."

He resumed pacing, but it was different. He was working through the issues driving him. And, more vital to her physical safety, she figured he wouldn't run her over if their paths crossed now.

Keeping an eye on him, she went to the fridge and put away the leftovers.

He began to recount what Steve had said. Steve and Annette wanted him to leave Nell alone unless she came to him.

"What're the chances she'll do that?" he said.

"One hundred percent."

That stopped him again. "You think she'll have questions?"

"I know she has questions. She's had them about her Uncle Zach for a long time. Being told you're her biological father raised more. And now that you've shown up, there will be even more questions."

"What kind of questions?"

"You'll see." And she smiled.

"That's not reassuring, Fran."

Her smile deepened. "It wasn't meant to be."

Fran heard giggling even before she turned the corner of Bliss House, and she knew, absolutely knew, that Zach was the cause. She remembered hearing that sort of giggling in his vicinity frequently during his teens.

It was a perfect fall day at the end of September. Warm with a crisp breeze. Sunny with occasional trails of clouds to break up the light blue expanse. The kind of day that made you glad to spend it from morning to dusk digging in the dirt.

She spotted Zach first. His jeans were drawn taut over his even tauter rear end as he raised one foot to drive a shovel into the ground. Then he bent and lifted the clod of earth, shifting muscles in his thighs, across his back and down his arms.

Her mouth went dry.

And then her field of vision widened to the gigglers.

It was the Tobias Garden Club. Half the women clustered around him were old enough to be his mother, the other half could have been his grandmother.

And she'd reacted like a jealous teenybopper.

How stupid. Beyond stupid. Stupid might apply if she had a right to be jealous. But, come on, she and Zach were not even in a universe where the concept of jealousy existed. It was the equivalent of being jealous of a movie star.

"Ready for the pansies, ladies?" she asked.

As one they scurried away from Zach like iron filings released from a magnet.

"Not quite," called Muriel Henderson from the far end of the garden. "A few more minutes."

Zach looked over his shoulder and smiled at Fran as he drove the shovel into the ground again.

"Are you done preparing for the shrubs in the Moonlight Garden?" she asked.

"Nope. Ran into a problem with the snowball."

"I'm surprised you've had time to run into problems."

One of his eyebrows hiked up. "Sorry, boss. I was trying to make it a little easier for your volunteers—"

"And lapping up their adoration like a cat with cream." She smiled to show it wasn't a serious criticism, simply a wry observation, but he turned his head away, apparently fascinated by Bliss House's roofline.

"I suppose I was." He sounded thoughtful. "I knew most of those women when I was a kid. Muriel Henderson, Miriam Jenkins and the others. I don't remember talking with them like that. In fact, I knew Miriam from when she worked at the high school and I used to get sent to the principal. Guess it was a novelty not being frowned at as the bad boy of Tobias."

"Not everyone frowned at you for being the bad boy," Fran teased. "I remember girls swooning over you and your baby-blue eyes."

He looked at her, and her grin died under that laser stare.

"But not you, Fran, right? Never you."

Before she could interpret the remark, the light in his eyes switched to low. A multipurpose beam she had almost grown accustomed to.

He thrust the shovel into the ground, took off his gloves and slapped them on his thigh. Fine dirt sprayed out and left a print on his leg like a hand curved around that hard, lean muscle.

"C'mon, I'll show you the problem with the snowball," he said, moving off. "That old maple has a main root right where you wanted to put the new bush. Could be why the old one died. I'll have to shift the spot, but any way I go will put it closer to the others than you wanted. So you'll have to tell me what you think."

She didn't budge until he turned back from the path leading out of the Grandmother's Garden. "Are you coming, Fran?"

"Yes." Coming unglued, that's what.

Friday morning, Zach was closer to the back door than Fran was when Chester gave her first excited bark. Also, he could see Fran was still trying to accept the reality that she was up and moving, so he stepped outside to see what it was all about.

The dog stood looking out the screen door, her tail wagging industriously. At the bottom of the steps Zach saw Nell leaning her bicycle against the railing. She was grinning up at the dog.

Then she saw him.

She stopped with one hand on the railing but both feet still on the ground.

He heard Fran behind him. She barely hesitated before moving around him to open the door from the house, cross the porch and open the outside door.

"Hello, Nell, come on in."

The girl's eyes shifted to him, then back to Fran. "I came to see Chester and her puppies." If she'd added *not you,* the message couldn't have been clearer. "Annette says I can't bring Pansy over yet. She and Chester are friends, but Chester won't like other dogs around her puppies. But Pansy thinks I've left for school so she won't get her feelings hurt."

Fran nodded. "That's a good plan, Nell. And you picked a great time to visit. Some of the puppies have opened their eyes."

"Really?"

The girl shot up the steps, greeted Chester with mutual delight then moved to the whelping box.

Zach had shifted his weight in preparation to leave when Fran's voice stopped him.

"Zach? Weren't you saying you wanted to see the puppies, too?"

"He can see them anytime," Nell grumbled.

"No, remember what Kay told us, not to have too many different visits from people these first few weeks. We don't want to interrupt Chester getting to know her puppies well."

"Bonding," Nell said.

"Exactly. So even though Zach's here, he's leaving Chester and her puppies lots of privacy."

Nell snorted, but Zach joined her and Fran at that end of the porch. Chester stepped into the box, threading her way among the tumbling balls of fluff, nudging two into a position that better pleased her. Nell knelt in front of the box.

"There's one. Look, the light red one has his eyes open. And that one with the spots. And that one, that's the same color as Chester."

"From what Dr. Maclaine says, they should all have their eyes open in another day," Fran told her. "Then they'll bark at each other and really start to move around. And we'll have trouble keeping them in the box."

Nell sighed. "I wish I'd seen Pansy when she was this little. I never got to see her until she was lots bigger."

Something squeezed Zach's chest. All the landmarks he would never see Nell reach. Walking, talking—hell, he didn't even know what else happened with a kid.

"You can help me take care of the puppies, so you'll get to see the stages now," Fran said. "But you don't want Pansy to feel neglected, do you?"

"I won't ever let her feel neglected. I only leave her when I have to, like for school." Nell twisted around as if to look at Zach, but her gaze stopped short. "Where'd you go when you left?"

There was no mistaking the challenge that bordered on condemnation. He couldn't say she wasn't entitled.

"I went a lot of places. Montana first."

"What did you do there?"

"I worked for a rancher."

"Like a cowboy?"

"No. More like a farmhand."

"Oh." He'd pricked the balloon of her interest. "How long did you stay there?"

"Until winter hit."

"You left because it was cold?" *What a wuss,* was the unspoken message.

"Because the rancher didn't need me to work anymore so I didn't have a job."

"Oh. Then where?"

"I joined the army."

Fran's brows popped up, but Nell didn't seem impressed.

Before she could ask, he added, "I moved all over with the army. Too many places to list."

The little girl considered that. "Where do you live now?"

"Virginia."

"Oh."

He had no idea how to take the syllable. It was not quite dismissive.

Fran said, "Nell, if you don't get going you'll be late for school."

Zach felt as if the bell had rung to end round one of a fight against the champion, and he was a definite underdog.

He and Fran, side by side, watched Nell ride away on her bike.

"After that, you shouldn't worry any more that she won't be asking you questions," Fran said.

He looked over at her. She was smiling.

Maybe he wasn't ready to focus yet on this first Q-and-A session with his daughter—if you didn't count their meeting at Corbett House, and he sure as hell didn't—because his mind zeroed in on something else.

Fran. She knew Nell so well. Far better, it seemed to him, than an ordinary neighbor would.

"Did you know at the time that Steve had married Lily to protect the baby?"

She gave him a look. It wasn't obvious, but he was pretty sure of what it said.

"It wasn't hard to figure out."

He'd been right. Her look had said: *What do you take me for? An idiot?*

"For starters," she continued, "he was in love with Annette. Second, the guy had been going around like he was in the advanced stages of shell shock."

"Because Annette walked out after Lily burst into their wedding—you told me that last night."

She eyed him for a second, and he knew he wasn't going

to like whatever she was about to say. "It started before that. It started when you left."

He felt a strange sensation in his chest, as if a huge blood pressure cuff had been wrapped around it and·pumped way over the limit.

"He was worried about you, Zach. From that first night you took off. Then when Lily came to him—"

"Wait, how do you know Lily went to him?"

"I saw them. Unfortunately, I wasn't the only one. Other people put their own spin on it. And some told Annette."

"But you didn't—tell Annette, I mean."

"No."

"You wouldn't, would you. You keep things to yourself."

He saw a tinge of pink deepen in her cheeks, but she gave no other reaction.

"Yes, I do," she said.

"So you got to know Nell after you came back to care for your dad?"

"Oh, I saw them before that. When Steve was in grad school in Madison, and I'd started at UW, I babysat for Nell. Lily wasn't around much, even at the start, and they divorced quickly."

"So what happened?"

"What do you mean what happened?" She looked puzzled. Of course she was puzzled. She couldn't figure out why on earth he'd growled the question at her. Neither could he.

What the hell business was it of his? None.

His brother and Fran had been in close quarters, united in caring about this child—his child. Steve and Fran and Nell…

"Why did you and Steve stop seeing each other?"

"Why?" Her brows arched in wry surprise. "Because we never started. You think Steve and I…? That's nuts."

Now it was his turn to be puzzled. "Why? You spent time together, you both cared about Nell. He had to be lonely— Oh, I get it. There was somebody else."

"No—that's… Oh, yes. You mean Annette."

It wasn't what he'd meant. He'd meant someone else for her, not Steve. Is that what had rattled her? Because calm, serene, cool Fran Dalton *was* absolutely rattled. But why?

Before he could probe for an answer, she'd regained a close approximation of her usual composure.

"There was never anything between Steve and me. The idea is laughable. He's Steve Corbett, for heaven's sake."

"Yeah, so? And you're Fran Dalton."

"That's exactly right—funny little Fran Dalton from next door. Even the people who don't live next door see me that way."

And she smiled.

Zach watched from the upstairs hall window as Fran's brother and sister-in-law-to-be arrived.

For the first time, Fran had agreed to stop working at Bliss House before she'd put in a day that would bring a stevedore to his knees. After a shower, Zach had made a run to the grocery store for items he'd missed the first time through.

Fran was in the basement doing something. He'd called out when he got back, but all she'd said in return was, "I'll be right up." But she hadn't come up.

He'd put away the groceries, prepared Stromboli for dinner and come upstairs to check his messages in Virginia. Maybe check in with work, even though Taz had said he didn't need to.

As Zach walked past the window, he'd seen the unfamiliar car behind the house. Then he'd noticed the Illinois plates.

Rob Dalton parked on Kelly Street. He got out of the car

looking weary. A woman with quicksilver moves popped out from the passenger side. When their arms went around each other's backs, it was as if air had been pumped back into Rob. Together they walked across the street to Steve's house.

"Oh, good, Rob and Kay are here," Fran said from behind him.

"Not here. They've gone to Steve's house."

"Sure. He's gone to see for himself how Steve and Annette feel about all this, and to give his support."

He faced her. She held a stack of folded clean laundry that came up to her nose. "What about you?"

"What about me what?"

"Your brother should be supporting you."

She clicked her tongue. "What would I need support for?"

He leaned back, looking at her. "How about for taking in the pariah of Tobias?"

"Taking you in? This is a fair exchange, Zach—your labor for the room and board. Now what are you smiling about?"

"You. You didn't argue about me being the pariah of Tobias. Forget Abe Lincoln, we should all remember Honest Fran Dalton."

She chuckled. "I'd rather be Abe Lincoln than George Washington—wooden teeth." She shuddered. "Hey, what are you doing?"

"Taking this mountain of laundry from you."

"I don't need—"

"Of course not, Honest Fran Dalton doesn't need anything. Humor me. Now, where do you want this?"

She huffed out a breath but quit wrestling him for the laundry. "My room."

He followed her down the hall to the opposite end of the house from where he was staying.

Despite the flannel shirt she wore over a turtleneck and jeans he would have liked to shrink a couple sizes, he could see the movement of her firm rear end and the slight, natural roll of her hips.

"On the bed is fine," she said.

For a nanosecond, he forgot she was talking about the armload of laundry he held. It was a very hot, very happy nanosecond.

He set the pile on the bed. When he started to pull his arms out, it threatened to topple. Fran reached across him to hold the top steady.

That scent of sweet earth and tart lemons. He turned his head to breathe it in more deeply. Her profile was inches away, the curves and angles of her forehead, nose, lips and chin creating a landscape that no gardener could manufacture. Her smooth cheek would taste of that lemony scent, if he put his lips on it. And then on her mouth and—

"I have to sort the pile. There are clean towels for you toward the bottom, if you want to wait."

Her brisk voice jerked him back to the moment. "Sure," he said, quickly straightening. He turned around. "Nice room."

It was a lot like her. Clean, spare, functional furniture that might be considered austere if not for beautiful lines and warming red tones in the wood. The pieces didn't match, but they blended, like old friends.

"Thanks. I've always liked Shaker."

"What's the wood?"

"Natural cherry."

"You had this growing up?"

"No, I bought it in Madison. Got rid of everything I'd had before. Fresh start."

There'd been a slight hesitation after the word *before* that made him wonder, *before what*? But during his early-morning run today he'd realized that Fran hadn't pushed into any area he hadn't volunteered information about. He couldn't do anything but give her the same space. Could he?

He wandered over to the padded window seat that faced Corbett House. He remembered seeing her as a kid, sitting in this window. He'd never realized what a good view she'd had of his childhood home. He wondered how much she had seen.

Then he spotted the books on the table beside the window seat. They were about volunteering in national parks, teaching in inner cities, and taking courses at about a score of colleges.

"Are you planning on leaving, Fran?"

He barely recognized his hoarse question, had no idea where the accusation in it came from.

She raised her head. "At some point. After all, I've been coasting these past couple of years since Dad died and I can't do that forever. I should get out, get a job like a normal adult."

"What did you do after college?"

"I was assistant director of a nonprofit that counsels troubled kids and their families, which meant I was a jack-of-all-trades: managing the office, fund-raising, dealing with the media, finding facilities in emergencies."

"What kind of job do you want now?"

"Something similar would be good. I enjoyed that. But the important thing is that the job gives me enough time and enough money to take courses. So something near a university."

"Courses in what?"

"All sorts of things. Not to go for another degree necessarily, just to explore—biology and astronomy and social science and Japanese and…"

Fran Dalton being fanciful. Who'd have believed it? He loved it.

"What else?"

"Criminology, psychology, more history of art, maybe the history of gardening and…"

Enthusiasm changed her face, turned the serene into exciting. Stirred something in him.

She ended with a shrug. "Who knows if I'll ever do it. Ever leave Tobias."

"You will. If you want to."

She shrugged again. "We'll see. Here are your clean towels."

He took them with thanks. Halfway to the hall door a thought hit him and he turned around.

"You know, Fran, there are all sorts of universities around where I live in northern Virginia. You should look into that area."

Right, like she'd leave Tobias and just happen to end up on Zach Corbett's doorstep.

She'd been bright enough as a kid never to fall for Zach or anyone like him, so no way was she going to make that mistake now, Fran thought. Look at what happened with Tim— and compared to Zach, he was a choirboy.

Chester's excited yips from the porch informed her Rob and Kay had arrived. Kay's voice floated up, greeting the dog. Fran had to smile. Kay talked to her pet unlike anyone else Fran had heard. A native New Yorker, Kay talked fast— not as fast as when she'd arrived in Tobias, but still fast, even to her dog. And she talked to Chester as though the animal was another person. Genuine affection in her tone and words, but no baby talk. And she left pauses in the appropriate places as if the dog might answer.

Fran reached the kitchen to find Rob and Zach metaphorically circling each other like dogs, and not the friendly variety like Chester.

"Rob," Zach said without moving from behind the counter.

"Zach."

Kay rolled her eyes and stepped forward, extending her hand. "Hi. I'm Kay Aaronson. And I hear you're Zach Corbett."

"Nice to meet you, Kay."

"Nice to meet you."

Fran hugged Kay and Rob. "What do you think of the puppies?" she asked Kay.

"They've opened their eyes!" Kay's face lit up. "You know, the next thing is they're going to be getting around a lot more, climbing on each other, climbing out of the box. We'll have to rig something to extend the sides, or you and Zach are going to have your hands full, Fran. And as the weather—"

"Fran won't have her hands as full if you're here," Rob said to Kay. "And Zach won't need to worry about it. I'm sure that if he's going to stay around any longer, he'll find another place. Somewhere more convenient. On his own."

Fran walked into her brother's line of sight, making him shift his gaze from Zach to her. "There's no place more convenient. Zach's helping me with the gardens and staying here, Rob. As long as he's in Tobias."

"Fran," Zach said softly from behind her. "Your brother's concerned about you and—"

"My brother," she said, not taking her eyes from Rob, "is being absurd. Half this house is mine. Even if you could run Zach off to stay somewhere else—and that's not going to happen—you wouldn't be doing anyone any favors. Did Steve or Annette say they wanted him gone?"

"No," Kay said. "Annette said she was glad you've given

him a place to stay and all of them time to deal with this.
What's that I smell cooking?"

As a change of subject it lacked subtlety, but Fran appreciated the other woman's support.

"Spinach stromboli," Zach said. "But—"

"You made spinach stromboli?" Kay's eyes lit up. "My
God, the man cooks, too?"

Fran's concentration on her brother flickered.

Too? What did Kay mean, *too?*

Surely she wasn't reacting to the famed Zach Corbett sex
appeal. She was in love with Rob. She had to be immune. Lots
of people were. Annette, Suz, her… Lots of people.

"Fran, if you need help that badly with the gardens, we'll
find funds in the budget somewhere."

Rob's words snapped her focus back to him, and the new
worry in his eyes. A worry that had to be strong to make him
offer to find more money in the strained Bliss House budget.
She would have to reassure him…later. For now she had to
set him straight.

"I have the help I need—Zach."

"That doesn't mean I have to stay here," Zach said. "If
it's—"

"It's settled. You're staying, and you're working on the
gardens." Fran gave Zach a quelling look over her shoulder,
then returned her gaze to Rob. He'd have more to say to her
but it would be in private and she recognized the signs that
he was beginning to accept that he couldn't change her mind.
"Everything's settled."

"Not everything," Kay said. "We still have to figure out
what to do about the puppies roaming around."

* * *

Dinner would have been as tense as a guitar string if it hadn't been for Kay Aaronson.

Zach noticed she talked about wide-ranging subjects that drew each of them at the table into the conversation, at least temporarily. If one person dropped into preoccupied silence, she set off on another topic.

The best one was Bliss House.

"So here I was, shooting B roll for a music video and the lead actor walks out, and Miss Trudi shows up with this guy—" Kay beamed at Rob and they shifted slightly toward each other "—to save the day."

"How'd you come to be doing a video in Tobias?" Zach asked.

"Oh, didn't I tell you that? My grandmother's Dora Aaronson." The renowned artist was the town's only claim to fame. "She insisted Bliss House was the perfect setting for the 1899 wedding I needed to shoot. Then Dora came out and— I don't know if you've seen the mural in the tearoom area?"

"I haven't been inside."

"Oh, God, you've got to see the inside—it's amazing. And so's the mural of Fran's gardens. Dora painted it."

"With your help," Fran inserted.

"A little."

"A lot," Rob said. "Along with working up all the publicity for the opening." He turned to his sister. "She's at it nonstop at my place."

"Everybody's going nonstop," Kay said. "It's going to be a great opening. I have all sorts of things to update the committee on at tomorrow's meeting. I can't believe we open two weeks from tonight."

"Neither can I." Fran sighed.

Zach saw the slight discoloration of the delicate skin beneath her eyes. She'd been working herself hard for a long time.

As he looked away from her, his gaze met Rob's. For the first time there was something other than wariness there. Now there was shared concern about Fran.

"All the more reason," Rob said to Kay, "for you to stay here instead of coming back to Chicago."

"As long as you're talking to investigators in Chicago, I want to be there, Rob." Kay looked at Zach and did a mini double take, then turned to Fran. "Didn't you tell Zach?"

"Zach's got other things that need his attention," Rob said dryly.

"Well, I'll tell him," Kay announced. "Rob discovered his firm—you knew he was in financial management, didn't you, Zach? Anyway, he discovered his firm was doing things that weren't kosher."

Rob gave a quick grin. "That's one way to put it."

"Rob gave his boss a chance to fix it," Kay said. "And when the sleazebag didn't, Rob went to the authorities, because it was the right thing to do. And they're going over everything he knows in excruciating detail."

"Must be tough," Zach said.

Rob met his gaze, then shrugged. "It's not going to last forever."

Pieces fell into place for Zach. "Attracting media attention?"

"Some."

Fran stood, picking up plates. "Ice cream, anyone?"

As she took Zach's plate she gave him a look that delivered an explicit order not to bring up the *No comment* phone call from his first morning here.

* * *

Kay Aaronson wasn't precisely subtle but she sure was determined, Zach soon realized.

She'd decided he and Rob should talk, and here they were, on the porch, with Rob rubbing Chester's ears into canine bliss and him sitting opposite, catching glimpses of Fran and Kay cleaning up.

Rob had said he'd help. Zach had said he'd clean up alone and let the three of them catch up. Kay wouldn't hear of it. Maybe Fran could have turned the tide, but she seemed to approve the plan, and they'd been shooed out to the porch.

"These gardens—" Rob cleared his throat and started again. "These gardens are consuming Fran."

Zach heard his worry. What would Rob say if he knew reporters were contacting his sister?

"I haven't seen Fran this excited since she left for college," Rob said. "She wraps it all in that calm of hers. But I can see it. And the hours she put in learning about historic gardens… After Suz asked her to be in charge of the garden renovations, she spent night after night poring over books, catalogs and magazines."

"Fran's got a good head on her shoulders."

"In a lot of ways, she does. But when it comes to helping other people, she doesn't know how to balance, how to hold anything back. There was some guy in Madison after she graduated… She lets herself be taken advantage of. Unless other people look out for her."

In other words, Rob intended to look out for his sister and make sure Zach didn't take advantage of her.

Zach had no quarrel with that. In fact, he agreed.

Maybe Rob saw that, because he dropped his head and resumed rubbing Chester's ears.

"I should know," Rob said. "Because I did it to her. When Dad got so sick—when he was dying, I left it all to Fran. Oh, I visited. Came flying in for a Saturday night, but had to be back Sunday to catch up on work, you know. The day-to-day, that was all Fran's. We got help in, but still, dealing with the doctors and his medication and the house, dealing with watching him slip away each day, each hour, that was all Fran's. She gave up her life to come back here."

"She doesn't regret it, Rob."

"That's beside the point. I took advantage of her. And when he died... I hadn't realized how much it was taking out of her, not until it was over. That's the thing about Fran. She holds on until she thinks she isn't needed anymore. But then...she was exhausted, depleted. She needed this time here. And yet now..."

Rob's telling him all this surprised Zach, and yet it didn't. This whole conversation was a warning. It was only at the end of that last bit that Rob had veered from the warning. Then he'd been voicing concerns he'd had in his head for a long time. Perhaps he'd barely realized he'd spoken them out loud.

"The point is, I'll regret leaving it all up to her as long as I live. Family should make life easier for each other, not harder."

"Greatest joy, greatest sorrow—that is family. A man I met once said that to me," Zach told him. As if that explained anything.

"Smart guy."

"Yeah."

"Do you have any idea what your running off did to Steve?"

And now Zach understood all the talk about family. Rob was equating how he'd left Fran carrying the burden of their dying father with Zach leaving Steve to raise his child.

"Some. But that's the difference, Rob. You knew what was happening with your father, and caring for him was something you could have shared with Fran. I never knew about Nell. And Steve's made it damned clear he wished it had stayed that way." Zach stood. "I understand you looking out for your sister, Rob. But this is between me and my brother."

"That's where you're wrong, Zach. Maybe you can tell me to butt out. But Steve isn't the only one involved. There's Annette and there's Nell. There's even your mother. And there's everybody who loves them. It's not just between you and Steve."

Zach was silent as Fran drove to Bliss House. He'd hardly talked since he came in from the porch last night and left Rob out there with Chester and the puppies. Kay had joined Rob. Zach had gone up to his room, and Fran had double-checked that she had all the papers for today's meeting of the Bliss House committee.

Now, as they separated inside the back gate of Bliss House, Fran asked if he knew what needed to be done today. He gave an uncommunicative grunt and headed off.

As if this weren't all difficult enough without Zach going mute.

Her mood lifted when she entered Bliss House. Max and Suz and their workers had kept the warmth of the old materials while opening the space with modern simplicity.

Other members of the committee were already there, talking together, but when Annette saw Fran, she hurried over to her.

"Fran," Annette said, a tentative smile on her lips, worry in her eyes. "I want you to know Steve and I appreciate what you're doing. If it's seemed like we were—"

"Don't give that another thought. How are you, Annette?"

"We're okay." She gave a small shrug. "It's just living with the unknown. Has Zach—I don't want to put you in the middle, but if Zach's said anything about…custody." The word came out ragged. "Or the future or…"

Fran shook her head. "Nothing, Annette. Truly. I think he's trying to adjust to the facts. But you and Steve are going to have to talk to him about it sometime. I think, maybe, if he were used to seeing you in more relaxed circumstances—as relaxed as possible in this situation—it might help."

"You're right. Thank you. How about if we come over tomorrow to see the puppies. All of us."

Bringing Nell would force Steve and Zach to be polite to each other. "Good idea. Where is Nell now?"

Annette's smile bloomed. "She and her friend Laura Ellen are having lunch at Miss Trudi's."

"Miss Trudi's not going to be here for the meeting?" That was unusual.

"No. She said she had a good idea of the progress from being right here every day, so she was going to skip today to be with the girls. They were chattering all the way over here about how Miss Trudi made them turtle soup last time. Steve and I can barely get her to try broccoli, but for Miss Trudi she'll slurp down turtle soup."

"Good day, Zach."

Miss Trudi stood flanked by Nell on one side and another girl about the same size on the other.

He said hello, then watched the mismatched trio depart. Nell said something to the other little girl behind Miss Trudi's back. From the looks the girls shot at him, they clearly were talking about him. But not to him, not approaching him.

How the hell was he supposed to deal with her? What was he supposed to do?

Over and over, he jammed the shovel into the ground. He'd get the biggest damned rototiller he could get his hands on if Fran didn't have a plant every other foot that she wanted saved. So he jammed the shovel in again, driving it to a satisfying depth with his foot.

"Zachary."

Recognizing that voice immediately, he turned over the shovelful of earth and broke it up methodically. As far as he knew, his mother had nothing to do with Bliss House. So chances were good that she'd come to find him.

"Zachary," Lana said again, "I want to talk to you."

He straightened and slowly turned.

"Now there's a phrase that makes me sure I'm back in Tobias."

She ignored that. Ignoring what anyone else said was one of Lana's best-honed abilities.

"You are dragging the Corbett name through the mud."

The laugh he produced had enough sharp edges to leave his throat raw. "Literally you mean? Because I'm doing manual labor? I've got news for you, Lana. I've done worse than this. Lots worse."

She froze to the outraged stillness he'd induced in her so often when he was growing up.

"You will not do this, Zachary. You will not make a scandal of this and disrupt the entire family."

"What the hell are you talking about? You're the one who said we should get a DNA test. How was that going to fit into your myth of a happy family?"

"That has nothing to do with—"

"Give it up, Lana. You wanted me to have a DNA test to prove Nell's not my daughter, not Steve's, not a Corbett at all."

"No. I—"

"What? Has she refused to fit into your neat little Corbett box, too? So now you want to kick her out of the family? Poor Lana, all these people named Corbett and not one of them's living up to your ideals. Well, give it up, Lana. Steve and Annette don't give a shit about Nell's DNA. And if they did, I wouldn't. I'd claim her in a heartbeat. My daughter. Still a Corbett. So either way, you lose."

He turned his back on her and resumed digging.

Chapter Six

His cell phone rang, jerking Zach out of a muscle-sapping, sweat-pouring marathon.

"Yeah," he snapped into the speaker.

"Vacation sure as hell hasn't improved your mood any, Zach."

One kind of tension eased out of his shoulders. "Waco."

"You're so pissed at me for talking to Doc that you're lying on a beach somewhere and you didn't even tell me where? Or is this to get out of helping me with the cabin again?"

It was damned tempting to take the out. To say, yeah, he'd left town to avoid working on his buddy's mountain cabin. "I'm in my hometown."

"Christ, I didn't know you had one. You never talk about it. Thought you came from a rock."

Waco and he were oddities in close-knit Virginia Task Force One. The members of their urban search-and-rescue team largely came from the same region. Tom Robert Hancock, known to all as Waco, talked about his childhood in Texas incessantly, while Zach had said nothing of his.

"Yeah, I've got one. And there are, uh, complications here."

"If you're pissed at me because I talked to Doc—"

"I'm not pissed. You did what you had to do. And I made the decision to come back here. You didn't. Doc didn't. Taz didn't." Even if the latter two had pressed him.

"If you hadn't been having those dreams…"

They'd worked on the cabin during a few days in late July, camping out. The first night hadn't been too bad. The second night Zach had awakened with that sick feeling in his gut. Apparently he'd awakened Waco, too. Didn't take much for Waco to put it together.

"I gotta go, Waco."

"If you need anything, Zach…"

"I know. Thanks."

He dropped the phone on the shirt he'd taken off an hour ago and leaned into the shovel.

Informal but businesslike, the Bliss House renovation committee members each reported on preparations for the opening. Max and Suz about which rooms would be ready, Annette on crafts that would be for sale, Suz about display spaces, Fran on the gardens, Steve on efforts to get another grant, Rob on the budget ("We could really use that grant," he said to knowing chuckles) and Kay on plans for the opening. That last item took up the bulk of the meeting since the date loomed closer and closer.

After nearly two and a half hours, the meeting ended.

Fran was halfway to the door, when Steve called her name. "If you could wait a minute?"

"Of course."

Rob slowed beside her as if he would stop, too, but Kay tugged on his arm.

The door closed behind them and Steve came around the table to where she stood. "I can't quite bring myself to say thank you. It's… But you did what needed to be done, Fran."

He meant in giving Zach a place to stay, in keeping him close at hand to sort all this out.

"Yes, it needed to be done. And everything will work out, Steve. I know it will."

Her certainty dipped a bit when she tracked Zach down to a diamond-shaped bed at the front corner of the house that linked the Grandmother's Garden in the front with a rose garden along the side.

Not that he wasn't doing good work. He was. She couldn't ask for a better job of working the soil than he was doing. She just wished she could shake the uncomfortable idea that each time he forcefully jammed the shovel into the earth, he was thinking of some member of his family.

"How's it going, Zach?"

"Fine," he said with a scowl.

"I'll go change into my work clothes, and help you—"

"No." A flutter of excited voices came from the far end of the Grandmother's Garden behind her, and Zach's gaze shifted. "I don't need your help. And you—"

He had dropped the shovel and taken off at a run before Fran realized he wasn't going to finish his sentence.

She spun around to see what had caused his reaction. At the far end of the Grandmother's Garden, Muriel Henderson lay crumpled, half on the grass and half in the garden border where she'd been planting pansies. Miriam Jenkins was squeaking her alarm, while two other women knelt beside

Muriel, and three more—including Miss Trudi—scrambled toward the scene from where they had been planting.

Zach beat them all there.

When Fran reached the group huddled around Muriel, Zach had his head close to Muriel's face, as if he were listening to something she said. But as he straightened she saw the older woman was unconscious.

"Did she fall?" he demanded. "Or did she pass out and somebody lowered her to the ground?" When no one answered fast enough for him, he added, "Miss Trudi?"

"I don't know, Zach. Rosemary?" she asked, looking at one of the two women still kneeling beside Muriel.

"Couldn't get to her fast enough to lower her, but she sort of crumpled more than fell."

"Good. Whoever's got a cell phone, call 9-1-1, then go meet them at the drive to guide them back here."

"I'll do it." Rosemary clambered to her feet, pulling a phone from her sweater pocket as she headed for the back of the house.

Zach put his fingers on Muriel's wrist, not fumbling for the right pulse point, as Fran always did whenever she'd done that.

She stirred slightly, her feet shifting. Zach gave a grunt that sounded like satisfaction.

"Is she—?" Miriam started.

Zach spoke over her. "I need sweaters, jackets, anything to cover her up."

He accepted Fran's sweater, folded it then supported Muriel's head with one large hand as he slid the pillow under it with the other.

He spread the offered jacket, three sweaters and Miss Trudi's tunic over Muriel. Another jacket he rolled up and slid under her knees.

Her eyes fluttered and she groaned, then started to sit up.

"Whoa there. Stay where you are, Muriel." Zach backed the order with a firm hand on her shoulder. "How are you feeling?"

"I…uh… What happened?"

"That's what I was going to ask you." He smiled at her.

"I felt a little light-headed, then…"

With that smile aimed at her she was probably feeling light-headed right now, too.

Fran could see Zach was watching the woman's face closely.

"How about now? How are you feeling?"

"A little woozy."

He nodded. "Well, just stay there for now, and that should be better. Muriel, I'm going to ask you a few questions. While I do, I want you to raise both your arms and hold them there. Understood? Okay, raise your arms. That's good. No, hold that. Are you diabetic, Muriel?"

"No."

"History of low blood pressure?"

"No."

"Good. Okay, you can put your arms down. Has this ever happened to you before?"

"Uh…"

"Yes," Miss Trudi said from the opposite side of Muriel. "She's fainted a dozen times I know of these past twenty-five years."

Zach looked up at Miss Trudi a moment, then to Muriel. "You need to have that checked out."

"The doctor says it's nothing. I just—"

"They're here! They're here!" called Rosemary, bustling toward them, with two paramedics toting their gear following.

Zach rose, going to meet them partway.

He spoke in a low voice, but Fran heard snatches. "…cool and clammy. Pale… Breathing and pulse good…leaning over to plant…didn't immobilize because…syncope… No sign of TIA. No slurring of speech. Has a history of passing out."

As the group reached Muriel, one of the paramedics looked from the woman on the ground to Zach. "You got our Muriel to a T. Hi, Muriel."

"Oh. Hello, Bobby."

"Okay, everybody, back up, let us do our job," ordered the other paramedic, depositing the jackets and sweaters in Fran's arms before replacing them with a regulation blanket.

By the time Fran matched the clothing with the rightful owners and calmed the Garden Club ladies, the paramedics had Muriel on a gurney they'd retrieved from the ambulance, and were preparing to wheel her out with Miss Trudi accompanying her.

Zach had disappeared.

Fran tracked him back to the diamond-shaped bed.

"You knew exactly what to do."

"Basic first aid. Learned it in the army."

"Zach—"

"Fran, I want to get this work done before the sun goes down. Do you mind?"

Did she mind getting lost, that's what was implicit in that question. And she did mind. There was such a contrast between Zach's gentle sureness in dealing with Muriel, and his savage attacking of the ground he dug now. How could she not be curious what was behind each of those attitudes.

But how could she insist on getting answers when he was doing the work she'd asked him to do?

So, she'd put on her work clothes, and she'd occupy herself at one of the other seventeen thousand things she needed to get done.

Because maybe, just maybe she didn't really want to know. Didn't want to get any more drawn into this man's life than she already was.

Sunday didn't turn out at all the way Fran had expected.

When she'd told Zach there was no reason for him to go to Bliss House today, that she was going to be there only a few hours, that he had more than earned a day of rest, he'd growled at her that he'd be there working as long as she was.

Or longer, as it turned out.

Around three, she'd found him adding manure to the bed the Garden Club ladies would fill with donated chrysanthemums in a geometric design the Victorians loved, and said she was going home. This time she got a grunt, and he announced he was staying. And then she'd understood why he'd insisted on driving separate cars. He'd been planning this all along.

Fine. Maybe he'd work himself out of the monosyllabic foul mood he'd been in since yesterday.

She'd returned home to find Kay looking miserable as Rob packed.

"You don't mind if Kay stays on, do you, Fran?" Rob had asked.

"Of course not, but—"

"Good."

After she'd showered and changed, Steve, Annette and Nell had arrived, along with Max and Suz, to see the puppies, but it was going to be a quick view for some of them. Steve and Max had arranged to drive Rob to Chicago, leaving his car here for Kay to use. They would have dinner with Rob in the city then turn around and head back.

In half an hour the men had cleared out, Nell and her friend Laura Ellen were on the porch with the puppies, and the women congregated on the couch and easy chairs in the family-room area with soft drinks and popcorn.

"Was that my imagination, or did they practically stampede out of here?" Suz asked.

"A definite stampede," Annette said. "At least on Steve's part. He was afraid he might actually have to have a normal conversation with Zach."

"No fears there," Fran said. "Zach's at the gardens, doing his best to work himself to death."

"Gee, I wonder where he got that idea?" Annette said, making a face at Fran.

"Hey, I'm here resting now, aren't I?"

"I'm still trying to get over the shock," Suz teased.

"Speaking of shock," Annette said, "Nell told me that Miss Trudi had invited Lana to have lunch with her and the girls yesterday while we were having our meeting."

"You're kidding—I thought Miss Trudi and Lana were archenemies," Suz said.

"I know. After the way Lana tried to get Miss Trudi into a nursing home… But Miss Trudi seems to have decided there should be a peace treaty."

"Lana will never go for that," Suz said.

"Well, apparently she did," Annette said. "And I was as stunned as the rest of you. Not only that, but Nell said Lana was *okay*. Which is the best thing I've ever heard her say about her grandmother other than that she employs a good housekeeper."

They speculated for a few minutes about what Miss Trudi was up to, but since they had no more raw material to work with, the topic faded.

Fran saw Suz and Annette exchange a look that probably communicated a lot between the two old friends. They'd been college roommates who'd gone into business together before selling off their successful company less than a year ago.

"Kay, if I'm not prying, can I ask how Rob's holding up?" Suz asked.

"It's exhausting for him, but each day I see a little bit of the worry and tension being lifted from him. He's going to be okay." Kay gave a short sigh. "I wish he weren't feeling quite so protective."

"I thought you'd worked that out," Fran said.

Kay sighed again. "I have a feeling we've just worked out the first, tough layer of that issue."

Suz and Annette nodded.

"It's like living with an onion," Annette said. "They smell and they make you cry…"

"But if you cook them right they're delicious," Suz concluded.

Laughing with them, Fran leaned out of the easy chair, stretching to retrieve a runaway piece of popcorn on the rug. She had watched each of these women find love, and she was thrilled for them. Sometimes, though, she felt a pang.

And sometimes the pangs felt as if they might turn lethal.

Above her the laughter stopped and there was a stirring as if the other three women were straining to see something.

"What in the world happened to you?" Kay sounded torn between alarm and laughter.

Fran looked up from her awkward position precariously near falling on her head. Zach, standing just inside the door, looked as if he'd been sprayed by a mud hose. His eyes were on her.

"Call it a rototiller backfire."

She straightened. "Rototiller?"

"Don't worry. Your plants are safe. Used it on the kitchen garden."

"Oh, Zach, you didn't have to do that. With all the plants coming in this week…"

"A little more work isn't going to kill me." He looked down at his clothes. "I'll clean up whatever I track through the house."

He strode off, and solid footfalls on the stairs could be heard.

And then the other three women looked at her—as if she could explain the man to them.

Now there was a joke—the idea that Fran Dalton had a clue to any man.

Nell's before-school visit Monday morning didn't catch Zach off guard the way Friday's had. Not only was he braced when he heard Chester's excited yip, he was ready with a cup of coffee to take to the porch.

He poured a second mug, wrapped Fran's fingers around it and tipped his head toward the door, inviting her to move ahead of him. They both knew Steve and Annette didn't want him seeing Nell alone. She sighed, but slid off the stool.

"Morning," she mumbled.

Nell said hello to Fran, who dropped into a chair next to the whelping box. The little girl gave Zach a quick, neutral look and returned her attention to the puppies.

"Can I ask you somethin'?"

She didn't look away from the puppies and it took Zach a moment to realize she was talking to him.

"Yeah."

"Why'd you leave?"

Damn. He wasn't as prepared for this visit as he'd thought.

"That's complicated. What it boils down to is that what I needed to finish my growing up wasn't in Tobias. I had to go somewhere else to find it."

"Daddy said he wanted me as his daughter even before I was born because I was part of his brother and he loves his brother, but his brother went away."

Zach felt like a pile of rubble from a cave-in had landed on his chest. Fran cut a look at him.

"And he said he wanted me all for myself," Nell continued, "the minute he saw me. Daddy was the first person to hold me. Did you know that? The doctor put me right in his arms."

"I wish I'd known about you back then."

"Why? I don't do anything exciting. Not like you." She didn't give the words any spin, didn't make them sarcastic, pointed, self-deprecating like an adult would have.

"Exciting, huh. What'd you hear that was so exciting?"

"You were a—" she tucked her bottom lip under her front teeth for a moment of concentration "—swashbuckler."

"A swashbuckler?"

"Like a pirate," she clarified for him.

He shook his head in bemusement. "Never been a pirate. Your—Steve always liked water more than me, anyhow."

She studied him, those eyes unnerving. "Annette told me Daddy was a champion swimmer. And she showed me pictures of him with lots of trophies."

"That's right. I bet some of his records still stand at Tobias High."

"What about you?"

He shook his head again. "No titles, no records. I wasn't in sports in high school."

Those eyes narrowed in a frown. "What about the dog?"

"Dog?" He looked at Chester.

"When you were a kid like me. You took that dog in Grandmother's house and it had muddy paws and went all over."

"Oh. Yeah, that I did."

Her face brightened.

He'd been redeemed, and he felt ridiculously glad.

"I found this stray digging in the big round flower bed out in the center of the front drive," he told her. "It had been raining like a—uh, a lot, and he had about half the garden on his paws. I was going to take him straight through to the kitchen, but he got away from me. And then I started laughing…"

Nell smiled. "And he went *all* over the downstairs, even the music room."

"I don't remember that, but—"

"Fran said."

"Then that must be what happened."

"And Grandmother was furious at you."

"That's true."

"Was that the first time Grandmother said you're a no-good black sheep?"

Another cave-in.

Standing at the front door of Corbett House, facing those intense blue eyes glaring at him…. *You're my no-good black-sheep father.*

"No, that wasn't the first time."

She nodded. "That's what Fran said. Fran said you were always in trouble with Grandmother."

"Uh, Nell, you better get going to school now," Fran reminded her.

Wasn't it interesting that Fran had remembered that episode with the dog from his childhood? Could it be that Honest Fran Dalton hadn't been entirely honest about not having a crush on him when they were kids?

But so what? A crush when they were kids—that meant nothing.

"I watched your face when Nell was asking me questions," Zach said abruptly from the passenger seat of her car as they neared Bliss House to start the day's work.

Fran wondered where this might be going. "Oh?"

"Yeah, and I could tell you had questions you wanted to ask, too. Go ahead and spit them out."

She didn't waste any time. "That first day—why did you leave your car down the hill, Zach? Why didn't you drive?"

"Wanted to see the neighborhood. Didn't want to drive past and miss things."

She looked at him, not trying to hide her disappointment at that nonanswer. "Okay."

He grunted and said, "I knew if I drove up, it would be too easy to keep going. It would only take a couple seconds to go past and be on my way."

So, he'd made it harder on himself to take the easy way out. Yes, Zach had definitely changed.

"Why did you come back?"

"The absent are always at fault."

"What?"

"It's a saying someone told me—maybe I didn't want to be at fault anymore. You know those twelve-step programs where they say you have to say you're sorry to the people you've wronged?"

"You're in a twelve-step program?"

His mouth shifted into a rueful grin. "I don't think they have one for being a Corbett. No, I'm not in any twelve-step program. But a guy who *is* in one found me and wanted to make amends for a wrong he'd done me. Maybe that planted the seed a year or so ago—the idea of coming back. I thought I'd make it better by coming here, setting things to rest. I never expected I'd make it worse."

"What had he done, the man who wanted to make amends?"

"He stole my bike. It was the last thing I had, and it left me flat busted and he knew it."

They'd reached Bliss House. She pulled into the drive beside a Trevetti Building truck and turned off the ignition. "Did you accept his apology?"

"No. No—don't look at me like that."

"I wasn't looking at you any way."

"Yeah, you were, with those big caramel eyes all gentle and disappointed, but refusing to judge."

"I don't know—"

"I didn't accept his apology because he'd done me a favor." That stopped her protests over his absurd comment about her eyes. "After he left me busted, I had to accept help from this guy whose barn we'd slept in, this great old guy."

He chuckled. "God, Elliott would hate to hear me describe him that way. He prided himself on being a cranky old cuss. After the guy took off with my bike, Elliott gave me a place to stay in exchange for doing work he couldn't do. He was on oxygen and couldn't get around real well.

"I don't know that I'd ever had a friend who wasn't looking for something from me, but Elliott wasn't. Didn't take any guff, either. Laid out what he expected and what he'd give in return and lived by it to the letter. After a few months with him, I started seeing things straighter."

"For example?"

"For example, that I had to suck it up and *be* something.

When winter set in he said I could stay on, but I would be marking time and I was too damned young to do that. So I entered the army." He laughed. "You should have seen your face when I told Nell that."

She couldn't help it. She'd felt as if the world had turned over and shuddered. Zach Corbett in the army. Taking orders. Marching in time to anything, much less a command.

"You...you liked it?"

"I wouldn't go that far. It wasn't the career for me, but I did okay after a while." His mouth twisted. "It was a rocky start. But it worked out okay. More than okay. Elliott had said it would be the making of me, and he was right. They gave me training, more courses toward a degree and some great friends. It was a good experience. I told Elliott that the last time I saw him, last January." She saw his sorrow, knew what he would say next. "I got out there a couple times a year, but this time...he was failing. I knew that, but I wasn't prepared when I got the call three weeks later that he'd died."

"I'm sorry, Zach."

"You'd have liked him, Fran." He grinned suddenly. "And he'd have thought you were the best thing he'd ever seen."

She didn't know how to react to that, so she didn't. "You left the army...when?"

"Four years ago."

"And since then?"

He looked out the passenger window. "I work for a county government in northern Virginia, across the river from Washington. Who'd have believed I'd end up like Steve, working for local government. But it's a good group. Finally got my degree last summer. Have a little house I'm fixing up. It's a good life, Fran."

She'd sensed changes in him, but nothing like this.

And through the amazement, Fran felt a thread of uneasiness. The Zach who had left Tobias would have been a lousy father for Nell. In fact, he probably wouldn't have been much interested in her. But what about this man?

And what risk did that pose to the happy family who lived on Kelly Street?

She nodded, acknowledging his assessment of his life, then opened her car door. Abruptly, she pivoted back to face him.

"Do you have a family?" she asked. "I mean kids, because—"

"No," he said. "Not yet."

At the look he gave her, a shiver went through her. This could be even more complicated than anyone else in Tobias knew.

Why hadn't he told her the whole truth?

Zach didn't know exactly.

He'd decided before he set off for Tobias that he wouldn't tell Lana about his life. He didn't want to hear what she had to say on the issue, and the only way to keep her from saying something was to give her nothing to say anything about.

He'd half expected Steve to be far from Tobias; he'd figured he would seek out his brother afterward. But when he'd set off, his only thought was to tell Lana face-to-face that he was alive and that he was done with the past once and for all.

The past will not stop speaking to me….

Clearing up the residue of his distant past, putting it in its place, so the recent past could settle in where it belonged. So he could move on to the future, the way the old man had said.

Fate clearly had other ideas. The past wasn't finished with him.

Maybe that's why he hadn't told Fran all he'd done with

what the army had taught him—he was afraid he'd end up telling her about the old man. And the dreams.

Kay pulled into the driveway fast enough to spurt adrenaline into Zach's bloodstream.

He rose from his seat on the porch steps and shifted his hold on the stick he'd been using to dislodge today's dirt from the treads in his running shoes.

A gray sedan that had been closely following Kay's car parked across the entry to the drive, and a man with the straps of two cameras and a tape recorder crisscrossed over his shabby T-shirt and protruding belly emerged at a surprising speed, considering his girth.

"Kay! Kay! I just want a statement. How do you feel about this guy you're living with being in the middle of a scandal? Is it like reliving a nightmare? Give me a statement! How does your father feel about you being with somebody who's gonna send guys to prison like your grandmother did to him?"

Zach started toward Kay. There was a haunted wariness in her eyes, but she didn't flinch and she didn't alter her pace as she headed for the house.

"What's going on?" he asked, once he'd reached her.

"It's nothing. Don't worry about it, Zach."

Right. He believed that.

"Go on in the house, Kay. I'll take care of this."

"Zach…"

He strode down the deep lawn to the guy, who backed up as Zach neared.

"I'm on a public street!" the guy shouted. "I'm on a public street!"

"If you weren't, I'd already have called the cops."

That seemed to calm the man. "Okay. All right. Glad you understand I have a job to do."

"You're mistaken. It's not all right, and I don't understand bottom-feeders like you. If you trespass, I'll call the cops. But understand this, I don't give a rat's ass whether or not you're on a public street. You're in my town and you're bothering my friend. You'd be well-advised to stop doing both."

He gave the guy a cold stare, then pivoted to return to the house.

"Hey! I know you from somewhere. Where the—? I've seen you somewhere. Heard that voice. Who are you?"

"Wrong again." Zach told his muscles to keep going and they obeyed.

"I know that face. I don't forget faces. It'll come to me."

Zach turned back, arms crossed over his chest, and glared at the weasel.

As he expected, the guy climbed into his car, still yelling how he'd never give up while, in fact, giving up.

With the car out of sight, Zach once more turned to the house and saw Fran just inside the porch door.

"What was that about?" she asked.

"That should be my question, shouldn't it?"

"I mean that reporter saying he knew you."

"That's not a reporter—not a real one, anyway—and he's wrong about knowing me. But why would a guy like that chase Kay? Is this connected to that phone call the other morning?"

"I'll fill you in," Kay said, stepping onto the porch from the kitchen. "Let me call Rob first, then we'll get comfortable."

She was as good as her word. Fifteen minutes later, they sat on the porch with Chester leaning against Kay's knees.

"So why was that tabloid sleaze chasing you, Kay?" Zach asked.

"Ah," Kay said. "So you recognized him as tabloid sleaze. I did, too, as soon as I saw him outside the cleaners. That's where he spotted me. My family was hounded by tabloid reporters when I was a kid after my grandmother turned in my father for breaking the law. I won't bore you with the details, but it had a lot of elements the tabloids love: famous artist, family feud, society figures, betrayal, big money. They were drooling.

"Most of the coverage of the investigation into Rob's firm is from the financial angle. Only a few are trying to pump this up to a scandal, then connect it to my family's history. This guy is one of them."

"You let me know if he bothers you again," Zach said.

A smile spread across Kay's face. "As tempting as that is, it's not necessary. Just now on the phone, I told Rob about our visitor and persuaded him I'll be better off in his building in Chicago, with its doorman and security. And with me gone, the sleazes won't hound Fran or anyone else here in Tobias."

Fran tamped the ground where Canterbury bells would bloom their old-fashioned colors of blue and white in front of the spiraea.

"That's it for today. I can't believe how much we've accomplished these past three days."

She arched her back to ease those muscles, and saw that Zach was doing the same. The move looked entirely different on him, emphasizing the width of his shoulders, the power of his thighs under his jeans.

"I have a new appreciation for Johnny Appleseed," he grumbled.

Plant orders had begun to arrive Tuesday morning, continued through Wednesday and today. According to her clipboard, they were down to one midsize and two small deliveries due tomorrow. They'd kept up better than she'd hoped. There would still be planting to do after Fred Buchell moved the donated trees into place Sunday. But that was all within her schedule.

The gardens were going to be ready for the opening.

They would give only a hint of what they would offer next spring and summer, but judicious plantings of pansies and mums, plus some late-blooming roses, would keep visitors interested.

"These gardens would never have been done in time without you, Zach." She wondered if working hard eased any of his frustration at having no contact with Nell or Steve these past days. It clearly didn't ease all of the frustration. One night Chester's low bark woke her and she'd looked out the window to see Zach jogging up the back lawn, apparently at the end of a predawn run. "Thank you."

He cocked a brow. "You're welcome, but somehow I think you would have figured out a way to get them done."

She smiled. "I'm glad I didn't have to figure it out."

A slow grin lifted the corners of his mouth. He stepped closer, pulling off his work gloves. "There you go again, getting a dirty face."

He brought one hand up, the pad of his thumb stroking across her lips.

He'd done this before, that first day. She'd wondered at the gesture, decided he'd been telling her to stay still, not to move or speak, so he could wipe off the dirt on her face.

She'd been wrong. That wasn't what he'd been communicating then and it wasn't what he was communicating now.

But…

That was as far as her mind could get. *But…*

He leaned in.

Her lungs stopped functioning, her heart went into over-drive, and her mind did come up with another thought:

Zach Corbett is going to kiss me.

"Fran? Fran, my dear?"

Miss Trudi's fluting call barely penetrated her mental fog, but Zach swung away.

"Oh, Fran, my dear, there you are. I have been searching for you and Zach to— Oh, my, what a magnificent canvas you have created of this garden. Why, it quite takes my breath away."

Having regained her breath—and her sanity—during Miss Trudi's fluttering speech, Fran jumped in at the first opening. "Why were you looking for us, Miss Trudi?"

"Oh, my, didn't I say? A delivery has arrived that Annette is quite certain contains the seed packets. We did not care to open boxes addressed to you, although we are quite eager to see the packets."

"Me, too. Let me get my tools…"

Zach beat her to it, gathering the fork, spade and rake and putting them in the wheelbarrow. He followed behind the two women with it, while Miss Trudi told him the seed packets were part of Kay's goal to spread the word about the gardens. When he veered toward the potting shed, Miss Trudi insisted he join them.

"Oh, good," said Suz when they came into the kitchen. "Now we can open these."

Beyond Suz, Fran saw Max, Annette and Steve sitting at a table loaded with three large boxes.

Had Miss Trudi purposely neglected to mention that Steve was in the kitchen when she'd urged Zach to join them?

"Here are scissors for the tape."

Fran took them from Annette, just as Zach moved into her

peripheral vision. Miss Trudi's hand was on his arm, drawing him forward.

"You better open that box fast, Fran, before these two explode," Max said, nodding toward Suz and Annette.

She'd hesitated, she realized, waiting for communication between Steve and Zach. There was none, and Max's urging got her busy. Eagerly, she reached in and removed...

"Oh, no."

One more thing she'd have to figure out how to get done.

"I thought they were supposed to be labeled," Annette said.

"They were." Fran saw that each packet had growing instructions stamped on the back, but the front was pristine, glaring white, with only a sticker tucked under the rubber band around each bunch to tell the kind of seeds.

Methodically, Fran checked the stacks of packets. They were all that way. Max opened the other boxes and shook his head. She found the packing list.

"It's the right order, all the kinds of seeds we ordered."

"What are we going to do?" Annette asked.

"We'll have to send them back," Max said.

Fran shook her head. "There isn't time. Not by the opening."

"What a shame," Suz said. "But that's okay. We'll get the right ones and give them out later. People at the opening weren't expecting them so they won't be disappointed, and—"

"No," Fran broke in. "We'll make labels. It's too good an idea for promoting Bliss House to pass up. Suz and Annette, I'll need your computer expertise, but we can do this. We can use the prototype I sent the seed company."

"You're right," Annette said. "We can make our own labels."

"Then it's just a matter of sticking them on. Everyone come over Saturday, we'll have pizza and put them on."

"Like an old-fashioned sewing bee. That's a great idea," Suz said.

"Yes, of course," Miss Trudi agreed. "Many hands will make light work. Why, Nell and her friend, Laura Ellen, can also lend assistance."

"I don't think Nell—"

"Why ever not, Steve?" Miss Trudi asked with the guileless look that indicated she was at her most dangerous. "Surely you aren't objecting to Nell joining because Zach will be involved. You are aware, are you not, that Nell has had conversations with Zach in Fran's company?"

Steve shot a look toward Zach. "I know Nell's been over a couple of mornings before school for a few minutes, but for a—"

"More than ten minutes isn't in your rule book?" Zach demanded. "You want to set more rules about when I can see my daughter?"

The word reverberated in the room like the tick of a bomb.

Steve turned so the brothers faced off across the corner of the table.

"I am Nell's father, Zach. Getting a woman pregnant doesn't make you or any man a father. All you did was donate sperm—as reckless as ever."

Fran thought Steve's words sliced into Zach, but he was too angry, too intent for her to be sure. And out of his anger came an accusation.

"You told Nell about me because you thought I was dead. If you'd known I might come back and foul things up for you, you wouldn't have told her."

"We told her because a child should know—a person should know—the truth. You must agree or you wouldn't have tried to tell me that Ambrose wasn't my father."

Fran held her breath to keep from gasping. But she was the only one reacting. The rest of them had already known.

Zach, still glaring, softened the slightest degree. "I didn't know how to tell you straight out. I should have."

"You're damn right you should have. But you were never the best at doing what you should have, were you?"

Zach rammed the wheelbarrow over a rut. But when he reached the shed he forced himself to put the tools away carefully.

You were never the best at doing what you should have, were you?

Hell, no, he wasn't. That's why he'd gotten in the trouble he had; that's why he'd gotten the reputation he had; that's why he'd left Tobias.

So why the hell did it hurt to hear it?

Miss Trudi had gotten him out of the house—he wasn't sure how. It was the least she could do, considering she'd dragged him in there and then pushed the button on the bomb with her *Why ever not, Steve?*

Zach had told her to mind her own damned business next time, and then he'd grabbed the wheelbarrow.

He turned, and there in the doorway of the shed, silhouetted by waning daylight, was a woman. Not Fran. He knew that instantly.

"Zach?"

"You, too, Annette?" he snarled. "You're going to tell me to stay away, too?"

"No. Not me, too. I only have a minute, but… This isn't only about you, or about you going away."

He gave a scoffing grunt.

"It's not just you," she repeated. "After the gossip about our wedding falling apart and Lily and everything, Steve is protective of Nell with everyone. He worried that I might hurt her, and when I first met her he came rushing in as if I posed some grave danger or—"

"You? But he loves you—she loves you."

"She didn't know me then—" the look she gave him provided a split second of warning before she added the final word "—either."

It still rocked him. His daughter didn't know him.

"Remember, I'd been away a long time, too," she continued. "I'd never met Nell until this spring. And Steve was right there, worrying that our past would affect how I dealt with Nell, that I might fail to recognize she's become an individual these past eight years."

Yeah, he got it. Annette was kind, but subtle she wasn't. She was saying he also had to deal with Nell as she was now. No rewinding this story to when she was a baby. He had to deal with her as a girl who'd had a father for eight years, and it wasn't him.

"I've got to go, but…Zach, you know you were surprised Steve was protective of Nell with me because Steve loves me? That's my point. Because he loves you, too."

Chapter Seven

Zach came downstairs to the kitchen after his shower to find Fran dressed in loose gray slacks and an equally loose black top with the slightest V at the neck. That irked the hell out of him for no reason he could put his finger on.

Then, with one hand on the counter's edge, she squatted to pull a pot from a bottom cabinet.

Two things happened.

The fabric of the loose slacks tightened over her rounded backside and she gave a half sigh.

His reaction to the sound eased his reaction to the sight enough that he could move.

Two strides forward and he grasped her wrist, lifting her hand from the counter, drawing her up.

"C'mon."

She looked at him as if he'd grown two heads. "What are you talking about?"

"We're going out." He tugged at her wrist.

"Where?" But she was moving.

"I don't know yet."

"But, Zach, I've started dinner and—"

"Is there anything cooking?" He scanned the stove. No indicator lights were on. He would have slowed enough to turn them off. No sense burning her house down.

"No, but I've defrosted a—"

"Throw it away when we get back." As he headed outside, he grabbed her house keys from the peg by the door. Fran pulled the door closed behind her. "Right now we're going out."

"But my hair's still wet from my shower. Your hair's wet and—"

"It'll dry. No more excuses."

That wasn't quite the end of it. She continued her protests about hair, clothes, wasted food and the general impossibility of doing something on the spur of the moment.

And the more she talked, the more determined he was. So he nixed her suggestion of the Tastee-Treat. She then set to convincing him they really weren't dressed for the Toby.

He agreed with her and drove past it without a glance.

When he pulled into the drive of the Tobias Country Club, her mouth opened, but no sound came out.

He drove up to the porticoed entry, flipped the kid standing there his keys.

"But, Zach—"

"No buts." He gave the kid a ten and went around to open the passenger door, reaching across Fran's motionless body to release the seat belt. Motionless but not ineffectual.

Oh, that body was affecting him plenty. Her breath on the fine hairs at the back of his neck. The closeness to her breasts.

The tender seam at the top of her thighs. A tempting heat that seemed to call to him...

What the hell was he thinking? Fran Dalton hot for him? It was his own heat he was feeling. Like a dog in heat. And he'd better get a grip on it. Fast.

Shock made Fran practically dead weight, so he slid his hand under her upper arm and half lifted her out.

"Zach, you can't—"

"We can."

He linked his hand with hers and led her through the front doors of the Tobias Country Club.

The interior hadn't changed. He supposed they must have replaced furniture, carpet and such to keep it looking so much the same after more than eight years, but he couldn't tell.

He led Fran to the discreet stand angled at the arched entry to the dining room.

"Two for dinner."

The man standing there turned back to them from contemplating the dining room—as if he hadn't spotted and sized up the newcomers the instant they walked in the door. And Zach knew at least one thing had changed at the Tobias Country Club. Walter was no longer Cerberus, guarding the gates of Hell, as he and Steve used to call the place.

"Casual—" The man sneered the word. Walter never would have been so obvious. "—fare can be obtained at the bar."

"Not the bar. The dining room. Dinner. For two."

The man made the mistake of meeting Zach's eyes and faltered an instant. Then he rallied. "We are completely booked tonight."

He said this without regard for the fact that two-thirds of the tables were empty. At the same time, Fran's shock apparently had worn off sufficiently to allow her to pull back against Zach's hand. He tightened his hold.

"Check again." Zach kept the order pleasant, but implacable.

"Zach…" Fran said from behind him.

"As I said," the man intoned, "we are booked for tonight. Furthermore, jackets are required of *gentlemen* in the dining room."

"Guy," said a deep voice, "I am certain that you can find a jacket that will fit Mr. Corbett from among those kept on hand for members and guests who require one."

The eyes of the man behind the lectern widened at the name, but Zach was more interested in the new arrival.

"Walter? Is that you?"

"Yes, Mr. Zach, it is." A twitch at the corners of his creased mouth was the only emotion that showed. "Guy."

At that quiet reminder, the man headed for the closet. Zach had rarely eaten dinner here when he wasn't clothed out of that closet.

"I thought you'd be retired by now, Walter. Off fishing."

Walter allowed himself a small sigh. "I had hoped to retire at the beginning of this summer, Mr. Zach—or, I should say, Mr. Corbett—"

"You should say Zach, no Mister."

"However," the older man resumed as if he hadn't heard that comment, "the training period for my successor is proving more protracted than anticipated."

"Let me guess," Zach said, "Guy was one of Lana's hires."

That twitch returned to Walter's mouth. But he neither confirmed nor denied—still a diplomat. He had to be to survive in this job. All he said, as Guy returned with a jacket that was less hideous than Zach had feared, was, "I hope you enjoy your dinner, Mr. Zach."

"Thank you, Walter. I'll come see you later to catch up."

"I look forward to that."

Guy seated them with acceptable courtesy and the waiter—another stranger to Zach—swooped in with warm cheese muffins, deposited menus and asked if they wanted drinks. Zach ordered a carafe of sauvignon blanc.

"Why did you do that?" Fran asked after he left them alone.

"I thought you'd object if I ordered a full bottle."

"I don't mean that." She flapped her hand—a most un-Fran-like gesture. He felt way too pleased with himself at throwing her off balance enough to cause it. But she had her calm back when she continued. "I meant all of this. Insisting we go out, coming here, pushing that maître d's buttons."

"The first part's easy." He tore open a muffin and smelled the moist heat, the tanginess of the melted cheese. He placed a muffin on Fran's bread plate, where she couldn't miss the scent. "I insisted you come out because you work too damned hard and then you go home and work more. No way in hell was I letting you cook dinner tonight."

"I do not—"

He cut her off. "We'll have to agree to disagree about that."

"Even if we forget that, why on earth did you come here? I thought you hated this place as a kid."

"Oh, I did. I definitely did. But I also know it has the best food in the county. Steve and I used to say it was the only prison made bearable by the food. No sense letting a little thing like childhood trauma come between me and my stomach."

He grinned. She didn't.

"Zach, as long as you brought up the subject of Steve—you weren't fair to him earlier."

"You mean not telling him about Ambrose? I didn't know how to tell him without sounding like... He loved Ambrose."

Her face softened. "Was that what you argued with Lana about?"

"Not really. She realized she couldn't talk Steve out of marrying Annette, which meant he wouldn't be her perfect Corbett heir puppet. So she set her sights on me."

Fran nodded, as if that explained something. "But I don't mean you were unfair to Steve about Ambrose or Lana. I mean that line about your being dead. It's what he's feared most. Right from the start."

Something in Zach slowed. "How about you? Were you worried about that? Were you worried about me?"

Temptation—at least he thought that's what he saw in her face—gave way to clear-eyed calm. "I had enough to worry about with the people who stayed here without worrying about one who…"

Her words rolled to a stop as a well-dressed couple in their late forties rose from a table kitty-corner from them and the man's voice cut through the room. "I agree with you one hundred percent, Jeannette. I've lost my appetite for dessert, too, when they lower the standards like this."

"Not even dressed correctly," Jeannette sniffed.

The couple could have chosen another exit, but they took the path that led directly alongside the table where Zach and Fran sat. And they continued telling each other how disappointing it was to have their dinner disturbed by those who didn't belong.

Zach pushed his chair back and stood in the path of the man, who was walking ahead of his companion. The man was stockier than him, but he didn't look as if he knew how to take advantage of that. Besides, Zach wouldn't let things get to that point, not with Fran looking as if she'd like to rap his knuckles, possibly with a hammer.

"Good evening," he said, in a low, neutral voice.

The man growled. The woman sniffed.

And suddenly Zach was grinning. "New members, huh?"

"Excuse us." The man exaggerated the phrase.

Zach stepped back with a wide gesture. "I certainly don't want to deny myself or the other diners the pleasure of your departure. Have a good evening."

The man glared, the woman harrumphed, but they moved past. Zach sat and encountered Fran's disapproving frown.

"That is exactly what I'm talking about," she said. "This is all about making a point—no, not even making a point. It's about making a scene that will get back to Lana. And you might find you haven't done yourself any favors by treating those people—"

"Listen, Fran, I brought you here to have a good dinner and relax. I'll tell you what, we'll make a pact not to talk about those people or my family or your family or the gardens or Tobias or the past. We'll stick to nice neutral topics like politics and religion. Okay?"

After a pause, the seriousness in her eyes eased. "Okay."

As they enjoyed their delicious dinner—give Lana credit there, part of her image was to have *her* country club boast the best food—they did talk politics and religion, along with books, movies and technology. For all her serene exterior, Fran had strong and well thought-out opinions. And she didn't defer to his equally strong, though, he had to admit, not always as well thought-out, reactions.

"I go with my gut," he said at one point. "What hits me."

"Getting hit in the gut can double you over," she shot back.

And then they were back to happily squabbling over which ten movies they would want to have on a desert island—assuming the desert island had a DVD player and electricity.

Maybe it was an instance of going with his gut, but as they left the dining room, he grabbed her hand and tugged her toward the back of the building.

"I have something I want you to see."

"Zach…" It was a question, a warning.

But he kept going and she kept following, even when he led her out the service door and down a path even more overgrown than when he'd been a teenager. The current crop of TCC teenagers must not be as amorous as he'd been, or else they had better places to go to make out.

"Here, put this on." He took off the jacket and draped it around Fran's shoulders. "It'll keep you from getting scratched."

The path widened slightly. The bench was still there. The wooden slats sagged under the years, but the cast-iron frame remained solid. He and a buddy had had one hell of a time wrestling the thing through the bushes to this spot, and there'd been a furor when Lana discovered one of her special benches was missing. That had made it all the sweeter for Zach whenever he'd used it.

But it suddenly seemed a sad and unappealing place to bring Fran—a teenager's make-out spot. Not at all appropriate for her, or even for him anymore.

"Is this what you wanted me to see?" Fran's voice held only curiosity.

"No." He tightened his hold on her hand. It felt good. Smaller than his, yet strong. Among the general softness, a scrape of hard use against his tougher calluses. "Just a stop along the way. C'mon."

He pushed deeper into the plantings, the one part of the country club grounds not defeated by Lana and her gardeners. The path barely existed here, but he was sure he was headed in the right direction—he could smell it. In another two strides he broke through, onto the first landing of the stairs leading down to the pier.

He positioned Fran in front of him, hands on her upper arms, so she faced the lake.

"Feel that? There's something about this, isn't there?" He drew in deep satisfied breaths.

"The lake?"

"Sure, the lake. But also that feeling of coming back out into the open, stepping free of what's closing in around you. Getting back to where you can breathe. C'mon."

With her hand in his once more, he led her down the steps, fast enough that she gave a laughing, protesting "Zach!" and clutched the jacket to her to keep it from falling. Then they went out to the end of the pier.

He pulled in another deep breath, feeling the coolness of the water on his face, smelling the familiar dense mix of water, earth and vegetation.

"When I left Tobias, I thought I'd never stand here again."

"You didn't *leave*. You ran off."

Cool and unflinching as a mirror.

"You're right. I did. I escaped as fast as my bike would take me. And found a world beyond Tobias, Wisconsin. But you came back to care for your dad, and now you help out by looking after Nell and giving Miss Trudi rides and taking care of a dog and puppies and restoring gardens. When do you do stuff for yourself?"

"Myself?" She looked up, surprised.

His chuckle was raw. "You don't even know the word? Here." He bent and picked a yellow mum from the planter beside him and slipped it into the buttonhole of the jacket.

"Zach, you shouldn't pick those. They're—"

"After all the flowers you've planted, you're entitled to wear a garden's worth." Going along the pier, he picked more—bronze, white, orange. "This is more like it."

He tucked one behind her ear, nestling it into her hair.

She chuckled. "If you think I'm going to put one between my teeth…"

But he'd already found a better place for the yellow-and-white blooms; he slid the short stems into the decorous V of her top. It drooped a half inch, an inch at the most, and he realized he was breathing hard.

She looked down, then up at him, and his breathing hitched.

But he saw only uncertainty in her eyes, the kind of uncertainty that said, *Why are you doing this?*

What was that about? How could she not see he was interested?

To remove any doubt, he brushed his lips across her forehead, then her cheek.

He thought he felt a faint dust on her skin. Like the vermiculite she'd had him add to some plots. Only this tasted like sugar. Yes, like granulated sugar. The sweetness from her skin, the grit from her garden.

His mouth found hers, and sweetness bloomed into intoxication.

She kissed him back, angling her head, answering the press of his lips.

His hands high on her arms, he drew her flush against him. The swell of her breasts pressed against his chest, one of the flowers from her neckline tumbled to the side and down. A small gasp escaped her, and he followed that opening of her lips with his tongue.

For an instant she didn't respond, then cautiously, she touched her tongue to his.

Who knew caution could ignite anything, much less a bonfire.

He plunged his tongue deeper into her mouth, and again. She met him, hands curled around the back of his neck.

Then she pulled back, pushing against his shoulders, turning her head away.

He released her immediately. She stepped back, looking away.

"Fran?"

Instantly her spine straightened, her shoulders squared.

"It's late. I need to check on Chester and the puppies." Her tone held all the usual Fran calm. But her hand trembled as she took the remaining flower from her top and the one from her hair and dropped them into the water.

She walked toward the shore. He matched her stride for stride.

"Fran, what's wrong?"

"Wrong? Nothing. I told you, it's late. I need to check on Chester and the puppies."

Reinforced concrete had more give than her voice.

What the hell had happened? After her initial surprise, she'd been in that kiss, too. Maybe even as much as he had been. And then in a snap she had turned as cool and distant as he'd ever seen her.

Could be she'd remembered what he should have been thinking all the time—he wasn't back in Tobias to explore this attraction to Fran Dalton. He'd come to clear out the residue of his old life so his new one could run smoothly. Then discovered a daughter.

Kissing Fran did not fit into those realities.

They climbed the steps, crossed a grassy area, then the patio, and emerged through an arbor to the front drive.

"Stay here," he ordered. "I'll get the car."

Not only did she ignore him, but she started laughing.

His first impulse—to demand what the hell made her laugh when he wasn't anywhere close to a laughing mood—died.

She had a great laugh—it changed her whole face, her whole body. She became a different woman. No, the real woman. The woman she had buried.

"What was that about?" he asked when she finished.

"Oh, Zach…" She wiped moisture from the corner of one eye. "I did try to tell you… That kid you gave the keys to— he's not a valet. His parents are that couple you blocked in the aisle. You gave your car keys to Tobias's current version of Bad Boy Zach Corbett."

This new breed of teenagers simply didn't have the energy of her generation, Fran decided as they drove home.

Either that or the kid had decided Zach's car wasn't worth joyriding in. Because when they went to the parking lot, they found the car immediately—parked in the president's spot, true, but with the keys in the ignition and no damage. The kid had kept the ten dollars, of course.

And she had kept her pride.

The laugh had done it. She hadn't known what to say as they walked back from the pier, but the kid, his parents and Zach's car had saved her.

She shouldn't have needed saving at all.

It wasn't as if she was a virgin. And she'd certainly been kissed before. Enough to know that kissing wasn't necessarily soft and pretty.

Not like this, though.

This contact of mouth to mouth could bring what was deep

inside, down where she hardly knew it existed, to the surface, creating something new between them.

No, what was she doing? She was making this into something it wasn't.

Zach had kissed her. That was all. A simple kiss.

It wasn't serious. Not like with Tim.

She'd thought she'd been in love with Tim—no, she *had* been in love. If she hadn't been, it wouldn't have hurt so much.

They'd met less than two months before she graduated from college, a romance that seemed to come out of nowhere. She hadn't dated in high school. In college, guys started noticing her. And she'd had dates. But none had felt comfortable or right.

Maybe a life of being an observer had left her with a shyness that was hard to overcome. Or, more likely, starting to date halfway through college meant she was taking baby steps when her dates expected sprints. And never the twain would meet.

That's what she'd thought until she'd met Tim. He seemed to simply enjoy her company. All that summer, with both of them starting jobs in Madison, they spent long, relaxed hours together. Until not only was she ready for kissing, she was eager for more.

They eased into making love. By winter she knew she was in love and equally certain he loved her. They wanted the same things—a home, family, children. Nothing flashy, no interest in conspicuous consumption. Their future together seemed clear and joyful.

And then came the night when the course she was taking in Art History was canceled because the instructor had the flu.

On impulse she'd gone to Tim's. His apartment door was open and she heard male voices laughing and shouting. Tim hadn't said anything about having friends over. She slowed, suddenly aware she had never met Tim's friends.

About to walk in, she paused, and the voices became clear. They were adding commentary to a movie showing on the big-screen TV that Tim so loved. She heard no dialogue, but from the commentary she knew it was porn.

"Does Fran perform like that?"

"Are you kidding?" came Tim's voice. "Hard enough to get her to do the basics."

"Then why keep her around?"

"It's not quality, it's quantity. She's so grateful, I can have it whenever I want."

Fran had fought her gag reflex. Steadying herself with a hand to the wall, she'd seen Tim's neighbor. A woman around fifty who always waved to Fran in passing, frequently calling her "honey." Now there was a pitying look in her eyes. The look seemed to say she had known all along what Tim was.

Fran had left without letting Tim and his friends know she was there. She hadn't answered his calls, which grew increasingly angry, until the last one when he'd cursed and slammed down the phone.

She'd been busy by then. She'd started by getting rid of her bed. The bed where she had made love to him and he'd had sex with her.

The first time she saw the Shaker bed she knew it was what she wanted. Once it was in place, though, it showed how wrong everything else was now. Maybe because Tim had seeped into the rest of the furniture. So she sold, gave away or junked everything in her bedroom.

And when her dad got so sick, the new bedroom pieces she'd slowly picked out were the only furniture she'd brought to Tobias.

* * *

He shouldn't have kissed her.

Each syllable of the thought was punctuated by a rhythmic footfall. Even after she'd laughed about his giving his car keys to that particular kid, she'd retreated from him in ways Zach couldn't define.

She'd gone somewhere else during the drive back to her house. Then she'd dismissed him with a few quiet words about taking care of Chester and the puppies and turning in early.

But she hadn't. She'd stayed on the porch a long time before coming upstairs. Only then had he slept.

Then the dream came. So he'd gone running again.

Zach stopped at the intersection now, even though there wasn't a car in sight. The streets were dark and deserted as they were every night.

And quiet, except for the voices in his head.

Daddy said he wanted to have me as a daughter even before I was born because I was part of his brother and he loves his brother, but his brother went away.

Steve is protective of Nell with everyone…he loves you, too.

…your being dead. It's what he's feared most.

Great, now he was having dreams *and* hearing voices. The voices of Nell, Annette and Fran, all telling him he'd been a bastard to Steve.

Hands on his hips, Zach rocked back from his waist, eyes closed.

Don't try to take on responsibility for everything, just what you're responsible for.

Fran's voice spoke in his head again. But it wasn't only her voice he experienced.

Damn. He shouldn't have kissed her. Or else he should have kissed her more thoroughly.

He opened his eyes, still bent back. A star like glittering confetti seemed to fall straight toward him. Was that the one?

Most hours in the disaster zone, day or night, it had been noisy, intense. But the second night there'd been one of those lulls you couldn't predict—hell, you couldn't imagine them happening during the controlled frenzy. But they always did.

The dust had settled, and Miguel said he saw a star, then added one of those proverbs he quoted all the time. *Stars are not seen by sunshine.*

Zach hadn't seen it. The old man made Zach put his head down nearly onto his chest, so Zach was staring up from the same angle he was, through the stripped bones of the building…to one star in a milky gray sky.

How many nights has that star been there and I never looked, thinking it would be there another night and another. And I was right. It will be there, but I will not. I go now, Zach. I go.

And he was right.

From habit, Zach looked both ways before he pushed off the curb, turning the corner.

The memories came with him.

Fran's voice drew Zach to the back of the house. She'd spent yesterday ignoring him and last night working. For once, he'd slept after his run. And wakened like a man with a hangover.

"Fred? This is Fran. About this weekend…"

Who the hell was Fred? And what did he have to do with Fran's weekend?

Zach stopped in the archway, making no effort to hide his presence but not announcing it, either. Fran was on the phone, her back to him as she faced the window. She and Annette and Suz had been up to all hours last night working on the seed packet labels.

"No. No, it has to be Sunday…. That's when I hired you for and that's when it has to be…. You agreed two months ago—! We have an agreement and it's your responsibility— No. How can you—? There's a word for it, Fred Buchell, but *business* is not the one I would use."

She hung up with a restrained click, pivoted smartly then started at the sight of him. "Oh. You."

That reaction was definitely a result of kissing her.

Zach raised an eyebrow. "More problems with the seeds?"

"No. We should have enough labels ready to put on tomorrow night. When I called, the company was apologetic—better than apologetic, they're going to give us a huge credit on the next order."

"So this is a different problem."

"Yeah. The donated trees." She sat at the table, casting a gaze over the battlefield spread before her. "The trees are donated, but moving them isn't. And suddenly he says there's a fifteen-percent premium for moving them on Sunday, when that's when it was scheduled for all along."

"He knows you're desperate."

"I gave him no indication—" She looked appalled.

"Honey, you didn't have to." He doubted Fred Buchell had picked up on the urgency in Fran's calm voice, but the guy had other ways of figuring it out. "Kay's PR effort's been so good he's got to have heard about the opening. He can put two and two together."

She frowned. "I don't have a choice. I have to give in. If the trees don't go in this weekend, we can't finish the gardens by the opening."

"I can do it for you."

She gave a short dry chuckle. "You are going to do it. You're going to be planting like crazy."

"Yeah, but I meant I can move the trees for you."

"Really? But—"

"Has he dug them up?"

"Partially, to give the roots a chance to recover."

"We can rent equipment to get them up and use the Bobcat to plant at this end. I know somebody who does a lot of that. I'll call him, get some pointers." He and Waco had moved a dozen trees by the cabin.

"You can really do this? Because—"

"I know, I know. The gardens won't be ready for the opening if I screw up." He pulled out the chair opposite and sat, letting her look into him. "I can do this. I will do this."

Before he'd left Tobias, few people other than Steve had looked at him to see what he had inside. But in his line of work now, he'd gotten used to it. Then there'd been Miguel…

"You really will." Fran's smile grew with each syllable.

He nodded, and now her smile was as big and bright as a sunflower. She grabbed the phone and hit the redial button.

"Oh, I'm going to enjoy making this phone call."

Miss Trudi bustled over to them as they got out of the car.

"Ah, Fran, I hoped you would come by today."

"She works herself to exhaustion here every day," Zach grumbled.

Fran frowned. He was getting as protective as Rob. "Can I help you with something, Miss Trudi?"

"I found an item among the books we had not yet catalogued that I am certain will interest you."

With the tight renovation schedule they had boxed the books in the Bliss House library, only separating those in the most appalling condition. Miss Trudi had insisted she check each book individually.

Now she held out a volume that had brown scallops on the edges of the pages, a spine that parted ways with the binding and something white blossoming across the dirt-colored front.

Fran lifted the back of her shirt to tuck her gardening gloves in her back pocket.

"You…" Zach cleared his voice and started over. "You should leave your gloves on. God only knows what's growing on that thing."

Fran ignored him and looked from the book to Miss Trudi, who for some reason was beaming. "What is it, Miss Trudi?"

"It's a journal my grandfather kept."

"His journal? From when he was planting the garden?"

She accepted the volume with reverence, opening the cover with slow care.

"What's the big deal?" Zach asked.

"Contemporary sources are always the best, and this might tell us the reasons for contradictions between the original plan and what's actually in the garden," Fran explained.

"The journal dates somewhat after the period when the garden was established, my dear," Miss Trudi said. "However, if you look at the entry under March 12, you will find something most interesting."

Behind the prim words, Fran heard excitement.

She paged carefully. March fourth…seventh…tenth… March twelfth.

She read aloud:

Winter blankets all beyond my window, although spring holds sway in my imagination. Even as I consider the offerings from the nurserymen that arrive in ever more proliferation, I received another letter from Mr. Jensen.

"Mr. Jensen?" she asked Miss Trudi.

"Read on, Fran, read on."

As has occurred many times in the annals of man, it has taken one from outside to observe that which is best in a locality. Coming, as Mr. Jensen does, from Europe, he sees and values what we overlook. His ideas spill across the page with an enthusiasm that melts the snow and allows me to see the garden that could be.

I cannot bear to despoil all that resides here, even as I see that it fades to old-fashioned paleness before the rush of these ideas. However, I will have a glimpse of this new vision beside the parlor, which has never been entirely satisfactory. Some may mock but I am assured of having the pleasure in the future of saying that I had the advice of Mr. Jens Jensen.

Fran's head snapped up. "Jens Jensen? Really?"

Miss Trudi nodded happily. "I found an earlier reference to Grandfather encountering a young couple not long in this country on a train as they moved to Chicago. They struck up a conversation about gardening and continued to correspond."

"Oh, my God. Oh, my God!"

"Who's Jens Jensen?" Zach asked.

"The father of the Prairie School of Landscape," Fran said. "It was a whole move away from Victorian gardening toward more natural settings. Jens Jensen designed parks in Chicago, not to mention the grounds of North Shore mansions—"

"And Henry Ford's," Miss Trudi added happily. "All that came much later than this correspondence."

Fran dredged her memory for what she'd learned. "My God!

This might be one of the first references to his development of the new style. This can draw lots more people to Bliss House."

"Scholars, historians and gardeners," Miss Trudi agreed.

"If we can find a curator—someone who would donate time. An expert on Jens Jensen…"

"Or the Prairie School," Zach tossed in.

Fran stared at him. "You're right. Oh—this might be another source of grants. We've got to tell Annette and Steve…."

Half a dozen strides toward her car, with Miss Trudi trailing her, Fran stopped and looked back. Zach leaned against the wall and grinned.

"Did you need me, Zach?"

"You know, I think Grandfather Bliss had it right about it taking people from outside to see what's really the best."

She shook her head—that made no sense. But she didn't have time to sort it out.

"I mean, you're okay with what to do next?" she asked.

"Oh, yeah. That I know."

Kay saw the journal's potential for promoting Bliss House as soon as Fran showed it to her that night.

Zach had cleared out after their return from the gardens. He'd said he was going to take Walter from the country club out for dinner and catch up. She had a feeling he also had some idea about giving her time alone with Rob and Kay.

Rob immediately went to Steve's house to check about the Bliss House budget. So she'd had an audience of one to tell about the journal. But Kay was a great audience, reeling off ideas on how to capitalize on the Jens Jensen connection to benefit Bliss House.

"Those are wonderful suggestions, Kay. No one else understood what this could mean. Miss Trudi was pleased, but in that vague way she has. Zach grumbled it was going to make more work for me. Even Suz and Annette didn't—"

"That's because he's nuts about you—"

"What? Who?"

"Who?" Kay laughed. "Zach, that's who. No—no, you don't. No giving me that Mona Lisa-plays-poker face. Like you don't know."

"There's nothing to know."

"Right. And—oh, my God, you don't know? Oh, honey. But…" Kay sat up. "Okay, you can tell me to get lost, because I don't want to mess up our relationship before we're even in-laws. But I am here to tell you that guy is nuts about you."

"Kay, Zach sees me as a friend, especially as the friend who's helping him get to know Nell."

"No way."

Fran shook her head. "You don't understand. Zach… Zach is…"

"What? The hottest thing Tobias has ever seen? Not to mention a Corbett. I haven't been here long, but I'm a quick study. I understand that. What I don't understand is why you think that would mean he couldn't be nuts about you. Have you looked at yourself lately?"

Fran smiled. "I don't hide from mirrors, Kay."

"But do you *look?* You know, Rob's given me grief about wearing black all the time. You could use a wardrobe make-over, too."

That surprised a laugh from Fran. "You don't pull your punches, do you?"

"Why waste time?" Kay eyed her. "Why don't you look through the boxes of clothes you're letting me leave in the attic."

"I couldn't wear your clothes—they'd be too small."

"Depends on whether you want to show your figure or hide it. The size you've been wearing is all about hiding."

"That's not—"

"Hey!"

Fran jumped as Zach called from the porch. Heat pushed into her cheeks, and Kay grinned.

"Hey!" He called again. "I could use some help out here. We've got runaway pups and I only have two hands."

Chapter Eight

Zach sat on the back steps, ridding his shoes of their daily portion of mud, when Kay came out with a sweater wrapped around her and sat next to him. She said nothing.

He finally looked over, even though he wasn't in the mood to talk. He'd been working all day at the gardens, getting ready for bringing the trees in tomorrow. He hadn't seen much of Fran.

She'd acted skittish last night, although that could have been from chasing puppies. Apparently all the puppies had figured how to get out of the box at once, and he'd nearly taken a header avoiding stepping on them as he'd come in from dinner with Walter.

Walter had had interesting things to say about Steve's leadership in bringing Tobias into the twenty-first century. And less interesting things to say about Lana mellowing. Right.

Zach had wanted to talk to Fran about it. But between

AWOL puppies and Kay's, then Rob's presence, there'd been no chance.

Today Fran had met with the other members of the Bliss House committee well past lunch. He'd caught sight of her with the rest of them, doing a walk-through of the house. Then she'd gone to work filling planters spotted around the gardens. They'd never been in the same area at the same time, and he had to wonder if that was a coincidence.

"I have a couple of things to tell you," Kay said now. "First, after Rob leaves Sunday, I'm going to stay a few days with Miss Trudi."

Why tell him?

"So you and Fran will have the house to yourselves," she added, as if she'd read his mind.

And now he could read *her* mind. "You're full of it."

"Right." She gave no sign of being the least put off by his comment. "Like that tabloid jerk was full of it saying he recognized you."

"He was."

"No, he wasn't." Before this could get into a was-too-was-not, she added, "You know, Zach, I'm disappointed in you."

That got him to look at her. But he kept his mouth shut.

"Even in the brief time I've been here," Kay said, "I've heard the tales of Zach Corbett the Wild One. But you're a total flop as the town's bad boy."

"You're getting your information from the wrong source. Try talking to my mother. Or my brother."

She shook her head. "I don't know about Lana, but Steve? He'd agree with me. Especially if he knew what you're doing now."

He went still. "What do you mean?"

"The task force, that's what I mean. Zach Corbett belonging to an urban search-and-rescue team that goes all over the world helping people. I won't tell them, but I don't get why you haven't. If you think Fran can't handle it—"

He laughed. "Like there's anything I could tell Fran Dalton that would disturb that serenity of hers."

Kay snorted. "Serene like a tiger."

"Fran? Are you kidding?"

"No. Are you blind? She protects her own. I was told in no uncertain terms not to hurt Rob or I'd answer to her. But she didn't hesitate to give him grief, either. If you hurt one of Fran's chicks, you'll feel those tiger claws. I know I'm mixing animals, but— Oh, wait. I've got that wrong." She gave a wide, wicked grin. "Unless *you* are one of her chicks. In which case, you're off the hook and everybody else better watch out."

"C'mon, that's—"

"No, you're right, I missed another element. You're still not off the hook. If you hurt her, then Rob'll get you, and I'll help. So, you might as well tell."

"There's nothing—"

"Zach, our sleazy tabloid friend remembered where he'd seen you, and in an attempt to win my confidence—a totally misguided attempt," she inserted with a blissful smile, "he told me. I've done some interesting Internet searches."

"Kay..."

"I don't understand why you're not telling your family, but I respect that that's your choice." She stood, brushing off her jeans. "But you know the one person you should tell, and now. She deserves to know, Zach. She deserves to know the kind of man she's falling for."

"I've had two great ideas," Kay announced. "Phenomenal, actually. I can't believe I didn't think of these before."

Everyone else gathered in the Daltons' family room groaned, but Zach noticed none of their hands slowed in the parallel assembly lines as they placed Bliss House labels on seed packets—one line set up on the couch, the other along easy chairs across from it. They'd been at it for more than an hour and weren't yet halfway done.

Nell had arrived along with a friend. She'd taken one look at him and declared she and Laura Ellen couldn't help because they had a school project to work on. Fran had set them up in her bedroom with a movie in the DVD player and popcorn, so he had his doubts about the project.

Fran sat on the opposite side of the room, as distant from him as possible.

She deserves to know the kind of man she's falling for.

Right, like Fran was falling for him.

"So what's the first idea, Kay?" Rob asked.

"We're not going to give the seed packets away."

"Yes, we are," Fran said firmly. "After all this work we most certainly are giving them away."

Kay laughed. "Relax, relax. I don't mean we're going to keep them. And we're not going to sell them, because I know the agreement you made with the seed company. And even though they didn't exactly keep their end of the deal, I know that you will. But nothing says we can't put out the seeds right next to a box asking for donations."

"That's a good idea," Max said. "What's the other one?"

"We need ideas to keep Bliss House in front of people after it opens."

"We've created a monster," Annette said.

Rob laughed. "You guys voted to put her in charge of PR."

"It's all Miss Trudi's fault," Suz said.

"Well, that's true," Kay said. "I'd've been long gone if it hadn't been for Miss Trudi."

Miss Trudi nodded graciously. "I am most pleased to be assigned responsibility for Kay being here."

"God bless you and your interfering ways." Rob smiled as he looked at Kay.

"Interfering? I have no idea what you could mean, Rob."

Over the chuckles that greeted Miss Trudi's comment, Annette said, "So what's your idea, Kay?"

"We're going to get lots of questions about the gardens, so we need signs out there, explaining what's in each garden and why."

"Oh, God," Fran groaned.

"You are the logical person," Kay said cheerfully. "You know what the plants are and why you chose them. You could add a bit of history of Victorian gardens and the connection with Jan Jansen."

"Jensen—Jens Jensen. But how on earth could we get all that on signs?"

"Oh, no, we only put enough on signs to whet their appetites for the book."

"What book?"

"That's the truly inspired idea. I told you the gardens will be what make Bliss House famous. You could put all the information in a book, along with photos of the gardens. We'll have the mural my grandmother painted on the cover and we can sell it."

"You're asking too much of Fran," Zach said.

He was aware of everyone staring at him, but the only face he noticed was Fran's. Her serenity rippled and ruffled like a pond in a wind.

"That—" she started. But it was all she got out.

The front doorbell rang. People looked at each other; everyone who was expected to be here was already here. And anyone getting up to answer the door would disrupt the assembly lines.

A ragged chorus of "Come ins" sounded.

The door opened, closed, followed by light footsteps.

Lana Corbett appeared in the archway from the hall, and people out-and-out gaped—with the exception of Miss Trudi, who sat there with an enigmatic serenity like a Wisconsin Buddha.

Zach couldn't remember his mother ever being in the Daltons' home, and from the others' expressions, neither could they.

Lana nodded at the group like a royal in a parade. But her imperious gaze centered on him.

"The weather is turning cool, Zachary. I have brought three of your coats."

Folded over her arm were a cashmere winter coat, a top-of-the-line ski parka and a raincoat with the famous lining. He'd rarely worn them.

"Thanks, but those won't fit me now. Better give them to somebody who needs and wants them."

He almost thought she suppressed a wince. If so, it was at having an audience to this exchange.

"Very well." She shifted the carefully folded garments to her other arm. "Zachary, I wish to speak to you."

"Go ahead."

"In private."

"After the past couple of weeks," he said dryly, "I can't imagine there's anything about us these people don't know."

Her stiff, expressionless face told him she wasn't pleased.

"Very well, I shall say what I have to say," she said coolly. "You have been cruel, Zachary."

"Me, Lana?"

"Yes. How could you go off like that and let us—let your brother—think you were dead?"

Zach looked toward Steve, who sat motionless, a label suspended over a seed packet, his head turned toward Lana. Zach couldn't see his brother's expression.

"Did you know that Steven hired detectives to search for you?" Lana continued. "That he placed ads in newspapers? Month after month, hoping for some word? And when no word came, he ran checks of hospitals and morgues and cemeteries? Did you know that? Did you?"

He had never heard his mother this emotional except for that day on the porch, the day he'd told her he'd be damned if he'd stay her son, the day he'd left. Interesting that she didn't know what he'd already told Steve and Annette—that he'd seen some ads, that he'd eluded the detectives.

"I knew."

Her hand rose as if to go to her throat, but dropped to her side.

"How could you…never to answer them…?"

All faces turned toward him.

"I needed to be away. From here, from…"

Lana drew herself up, head high. "From me."

He didn't look away. "Yes. From you. And from what you demanded I be."

"You are a Corbett. You have a responsibility, an obligation."

"Responsibility? Obligation? Why? For being born into this family? For that I'm supposed to abdicate any thought of being myself or deciding what I want my life to be? Like hell."

"Your father—"

"No, don't lay this on Ambrose. This is all you, Lana. Always has been. Some bizarre cult of the Corbetts that exists more in your mind than anywhere else. Why it's so damned important to you I'll never—"

"To make Ambrose proud." Her voice rose. "To give him the one thing I could give him after all he'd given me."

Silence dropped onto the room. And with it, Lana Corbett's icy control returned. With perfect posture she pivoted. She reached toward the table behind the sofa, as if she might steady herself, but snatched her hand back without touching it. Only after she'd turned down the hall out of sight did Zach realize that her hand had been shaking.

He became aware of the room slowly digging out of its shock.

"Only you can make that woman fall apart, Zach," Steve muttered.

"That is not fair, Steve," Fran snapped.

Every eye went to her. Color marked her cheeks, and she sat straighter. Zach's mouth twitched. His calm, cool Fran had some serious fangs. Maybe Kay was right about her being a tiger underneath.

Steve stared at her as if she'd grown another head along with the fangs. Miss Trudi took a sip from her teacup, but he thought he'd seen her smile.

Annette stepped into the breach.

"Steve didn't mean that as criticism, I'm sure. Did you, Steve?" At her prompting, Steve came back to life.

"No—no, I didn't mean… It's that the only times I've ever known my mother to lose her temper have been with Zach. And that's a skill—to make Lana Corbett lose her temper and be honest."

"That sounds almost as if you envy Zach the ability," Fran said.

Zach stared at her. What the hell? Steve envying him?

"You might be right," Steve said.

This time the silence was the uncomfortable kind that came when people have said or heard too much.

Suz was the one to break it. "We better get back into gear or we'll never finish this."

In a flurry of relief, they returned to their assembly lines. But Zach caught sight of a shadow flitting across the darkened kitchen area. A shadow about the size of a nearly eight-year-old who'd been listening to everything.

Rob and Kay headed upstairs after helping with the cleanup, giving Fran her opportunity.

"Zach, I'd like to talk to you."

"Seems like you've been doing your best to avoid talking to me."

Protests and denials bubbled up. She pushed them back where they belonged. "We can sit on the porch."

"Okay." He stopped at the door. "You need a jacket or something." He'd taken the trash out and still wore a denim jacket.

Swallowing the temptation to argue, she took an old barn coat from a peg inside the basement door.

On the porch she sat on the loveseat beside the whelping box and gestured for him to sit across from her. He sat beside her on the loveseat instead. She refused to let that dent her calm determination.

"I'd like to talk to you about something that happened tonight."

"If it's about Lana—"

"It's not. Although you were very hard on her, Zach. Maybe you have some justification for being cruel after the way she treated you growing up, but what does it accomplish? And if she was doing what she thought was best…" She let it die, because of his mulish expression and because she had something else to say. "But that isn't why I asked to talk with you."

"Good. It's too nice a night to talk about Lana."

Since it was cool and damp, she suspected he considered any night too nice to talk about his mother.

"What I want to talk to you about was your jumping into the conversation about the garden book and—"

"They're asking too much of you. You should tell them no."

"Don't you tell me what I should and shouldn't say yes to. That's exactly what I want to tell you not to do. You're as bad as Rob."

"What does Rob say you shouldn't say yes to?"

"I'm not going to get into that with you."

"Because you know I'll agree with him?"

"I don't care if you and Rob and all of Wisconsin line up and agree—I'll decide what I want in my life."

"Okay. What do you want?"

He'd handed her an opening. She wouldn't be passive Fran waiting for him to walk away. She would say the words that would send Zach Corbett running for the hills.

Before she could get any more foolish ideas.

She cleared her throat and wet her lips, but his gaze dropped to her mouth. She had to start over. This time without looking at him. If she didn't see his eyes, it wouldn't matter if he looked at her mouth.

Except that his look had left a sparkling tingle on her lips, and she desperately wanted to slide her tongue over them again to taste it.

Nonsense. Absolute nonsense.

"I'll tell you what I want, Zach Corbett. I want a baby." There, she'd said it. "I want several babies. I want to be a mother."

"And a wife? Do you want to be a wife? Does a husband fit into this?"

"Yes." She said it fast. No turning back. "I want a husband, too. And I might just want a white picket fence."

She waited. She had the strangest feeling he was waiting for something, too. But what? She'd said her piece. He should be backing out the door, if not running full tilt. Instead he sat and looked at her.

She sat up straighter. "So what have you got to say to that?"

"Sounds like good things to want."

"Is…is that all you have to say?"

"Well." He drawled the word out the way he did sometimes now. "I might mention there are a fair number of picket fences in Virginia."

Though her lips parted, no sound came out.

He brushed two fingers into the hair at her temples, his eyes trained on the movement as the strands slid free. She shivered as the ends tickled her skin.

"Zach…"

He feathered his fingers down the side of her throat.

"Hmm?" he murmured against the sensitive skin below her ear.

"You don't… I want you to know I understand. Coming home, your family, finding out about Nell. All of it. I understand."

"What are you talking about?" He kissed her forehead, then under the hair at her temple.

"And if you're grateful because I've helped out in any way…"

He cupped her jaw, slid his hand into her hair. "Just once, could you be a little less reasonable, a little less calm."

"I don't—"

"Shh."

Zach held her gaze for a heartbeat, then slowly looked down at her mouth. He dipped his head and kissed her.

It wasn't like the first kiss. She knew what he intended this time. There should have been no shock.

There was. Shock of joy and heat and longing.

His mouth covered hers with slow, sweet persuasion. She parted her lips, wanting the deeper connection. He answered her wanting with long explorations of taste and texture. The stroke of his tongue against hers strummed a moan from her.

Her fingers felt the soft hair at the back of his neck, sliding into the thickness.

They were both breathing hard now. He placed his palm on her collarbone, as if to calm her breathing. It did the opposite. The top buttons of her shirt had opened somehow…his hand slipped lower.

She was in some strange divided place. Wherever he touched her or she touched him, nerves and flesh pulsed with hypersensitivity, the sensation like a fist at the base of her belly that opened and closed. Yet languor claimed the remainder of her, body and mind.

"Fran…Fran…"

She put her arm farther around his shoulders, holding him to her. But he was soothing her, easing her away.

Oh, God, what had she done? What had she wanted to do? She turned her face away, and he stroked her cheek.

"Fran, this isn't—"

"No, of course not. I didn't—I understand. Good night, Zach."

Holding her jacket together at her throat, she was up and inside in a second. But she forced herself to walk at a normal pace to the stairs, not looking back.

* * *

To Fran's hazy, waking mind, her bed seemed to be on fire. The mists rose quickly and she knew it wasn't the bed at all, but the memories of last night stirring in her body that generated the heat.

She hurried into a cool shower.

She'd have to assure Zach that she wouldn't jump him.

But first she had work to do. This was the day they would move the trees descended from Bliss House's original plantings. No wonder her adrenaline was rushing.

After making the bed and dressing in record time, she pulled on her navy sweater over a striped shirt.

She turned to the mirror and stilled.

Was Kay right? Did she dress to hide? With a fistful of material at her waist, she pulled the sweater taut. She released the fist, then pulled the right seam wide so the left side snugged against her. Her right arm was almost straight out.

The material cupped around her breasts and emphasized the difference between them and her midriff.

She'd been late to develop. But when she'd started, she'd developed quickly. Overnight, it had seemed, because she hadn't paid attention with her mother dying that fall and winter.

The first warm day of spring, eight days after her mother's funeral, she'd worn a knit top from the year before.

Even through the numbness of grief, the reaction of the boys at school had penetrated. It shoved her onto center stage, when she had craved invisibility.

The next day she had worn one of Rob's shirts.

She supposed she'd found a more durable solution by gaining weight. Although what she'd told Zach was true—feeding and eating with Rob and their father had packed on pounds.

But even when she'd lost the extra weight, she'd continued wearing clothes that were too big for her.

This had nothing to do with Zach, only with her feelings about herself.

She shed the sweater and shirt, then pulled out a turtleneck she usually wore under sweaters.

The image in the mirror had her digging in a drawer for a pullover. Then she caught another image—her holding the sweater in front of her like a lifesaver.

She dropped the sweater on the chest and walked out.

Steve muttered a curse from the other side of the root ball they were wrapping in burlap.

Zach looked over his shoulder to see what had got the rise out of Steve, when he noticed Fran coming from the house, where they'd sent her to talk to the lady donating the trees. That diversion hadn't lasted nearly long enough.

Fran wore an outfit he'd never seen her in before. A dark green turtleneck that followed her curves and tan slacks that, instead of flapping around her legs, skimmed their contours.

Not ordinarily a sight to cause any man to curse, except she'd been driving them all nuts for the past three hours with her calm questions and just-to-be-sure reminders. She'd been driving Zach nuts for considerably longer for different reasons.

Last night…last night he'd been an idiot. Maybe it was partly excusable, because she'd been so damn-the-torpedoes, full-speed-ahead about her list of wants. As if she wasn't likely to get them, but she refused to pretend she didn't want them.

What the hell could he do but kiss her after that? And what chance did he have of not wanting more once he'd kissed her? He'd wanted more all right. If there'd been the least doubt it ended when she did that automatic slowing of the porch door with her backside on her way inside.

Yeah, he'd wanted it all. All of her and all her dreams.

But the one thing she didn't want, and sure as hell didn't need, was a bad boy, possibly reformed or not, but definitely screwed up.

"Max, go talk to her and keep her from coming over here," Steve said.

Zach held an edge of burlap in place while Steve prepared to secure it. Max's section was fastened, so he was free.

"Tell her we need her to go ahead to Bliss House and make sure everything's set," Steve added. "Tell her we'll convoy the trees and we'll be right behind her."

"It'll take a couple of hours," Zach said.

"In a couple of hours," Max repeated.

"No!" Steve and Zach chorused.

"Don't tell her that long," Steve warned, "or she'll stay here."

Max chuckled, and headed for Fran.

She looked amazing. When she'd come into the kitchen this morning, Zach had nearly choked on his coffee. That had turned her cheeks pink, brought a frown to Rob's face and a smile to Kay's. But Fran hadn't met his eyes.

"Max seems like a good guy to have as a brother-in-law," Zach said, mostly to take his mind off the view and the memories.

"The best."

"But he wasn't happy that you and Annette were going to get married before she finished school eight years ago."

"No. And he was a hell of a lot less happy after what happened at the wedding," Steve said dryly. "I went to try to talk to Annette and he punched my lights out."

Zach winced. A punch from Max was not to be taken lightly.

"But after a while, crossing paths around town, we reached a truce. Now, all he wants is for Annette to be happy, and that puts us on the same team."

"He should give you credit—you never stopped loving Annette."

"Not really. Until this spring, I had myself pretty well fooled I was over her. Hell, for a while, I was on a campaign to find a wife and…"

Zach pretended he didn't notice Steve stop short of the word *mother*.

"Couldn't find anyone brave enough to face Lana as a mother-in-law?"

"Didn't get that far. I only talked to one person about the idea of marriage, and if Fran hadn't been wise enough to see—"

"Fran?"

Steve gave him a hard-eyed look. "You think you're the only one who sees how great Fran is?"

"You and Fran? She said…" What exactly had she said? *There was never anything between Steve and me. The idea is laughable. He's Steve Corbett, for heaven's sake.*

"That she turned me down flat? Gently, but still flat. Said we didn't love each other, and a marriage that lacked the foundation of love was wrong for Nell. And she was right."

"You asked her to marry you." Zach wrenched the last corner of burlap into place and nodded for Steve to wrap the closure around it.

"Didn't have a chance. She cut me off, made me see I was asking for the wrong reasons."

What would Fran consider the right reasons? If she turned down Saint Steven, what kind of guy would Fran ever say yes to?

He tuned back in to Steve to realize his brother had just finished a long speech and Zach had missed all of it except for the final four words: "…too hard on her."

"What?"

"You heard me. You're too hard on Mother." Steve gave him the grim-older-brother look. "I know that growing up she gave you a hard—"

Zach emitted a sarcastic "huh." "I didn't grow up here. Didn't grow up until I left. When I was here, I was just a puppet to Lana's ambitions. That's all anyone is to her."

"I'm not so sure about that. Annette's made me see things differently—that maybe in her own way Mother wanted the best for us. If Annette can see this from a different angle, I figure I can try, too."

"Not me. Now let's get this thing in the truck and start on the next one or Fran will have our hides."

Fran walked to the end of the driveway and looked both ways. No sign of a convoy carrying precious trees.

Where was he? They—where were *they?*

She paced back to the seat built into the patio's brick wall where Miss Trudi sat. The rest of the committee and a half-dozen volunteers were inside cleaning.

"They should be here by now," Fran muttered.

"My dear, I'm certain they are all safe," Miss Trudi said.

Safe? She hadn't been thinking about safety. At least not of Zach and the others. The safety of the trees was another matter.

"You think—?"

"No," Miss Trudi said firmly. "That is precisely what I said. I do not believe there is any reason to be concerned for their safety. They are three remarkably responsible young men."

Well, two of them were. But Zach…? Had he truly

changed? Was she letting other factors cloud her judgment? Perhaps she had from the first. There was no denying now that she was physically attracted to him.

"If there were a problem of any consequence," Miss Trudi continued, "they would most certainly contact you."

"I don't know Zach's cell number or I'd call." She'd restrained herself from calling Steve's or Max's cell numbers. So far. "I don't usually worry like this."

"Indeed you do, my dear."

That snapped her head around. "What do you mean?"

"A few short weeks ago you were quite concerned about the growing relationship between your brother and Kay, were you not?"

"Well, yes. Naturally, I was concerned. Rob was afraid of getting hurt again, and—"

"I saw no indication of such a fear from Rob. Was that his fear or yours?"

Fran felt as if she'd received a mild electrical shock. Had she transferred her own feelings to Rob's relationship with Kay? And that question led to an even more soul-searching one: *Was* she afraid of being hurt again?

Was she afraid of making another mistake about a man the way she had with Tim? Was that coloring her reactions to Zach?

But if an ordinary guy like Tim could use her and be so dismissive, wasn't there more danger of that with Zach?

"They're here, my dear. You need to clear the drive."

Fran moved aside quickly, standing next to the Bobcat that would carry the trees to their new homes around the property. Max, the trees in the bed of his pickup, backed in.

Zach swung out of the passenger side of Max's truck and strode toward her.

"Where have you been?" she demanded. "It's way past—"

"There was a wreck on the Interstate—"

"The Interstate? I told you to take the back roads."

"We did, Fran," said Max. "But so did everybody else trying to get away from the wreck on the Interstate."

She'd been an idiot. She glanced at Zach. He was fiddling with the Bobcat's controls, with no effect that she could see.

"And what with being delayed, we took the rental equipment back first so we wouldn't be charged an extra day," Max added. "We tried to call, but you weren't answering."

"My phone never rang. Miss Trudi can verify that. And the battery's fine, so—" Extending the phone to demonstrate the battery's state, she noticed it had a black stripe down the side rather than blue. "Oh, God. This is your phone, Zach. I must have grabbed it off the counter this morning. Mine must still be there. I'm sorry. I shouldn't have snapped. I was…" She would *not* make the excuse of being worried about trees. "I'm sorry."

She looked up to find Steve, Max and Miss Trudi watching her and Zach.

He'd made her a promise, and she'd made it clear she hadn't trusted that promise. He knew it, she knew it and the others sensed it.

"Well," Max said. "Let's get these trees in the ground."

Steve passed Zach, still focused on the contraption's controls, and said something. Zach looked up. Able to see only Steve's face, Fran was still certain the brothers had made full eye contact. Not in anger or challenge or assessment, but in full accord for the first time since Zach's return.

Great. She'd given the Corbetts something to bond over—finding her a pain in the ass.

Chapter Nine

With the trees in place, Zach took a break to wolf down a sandwich and water.

He was sitting on Bliss House's front steps when the door opened behind him. Annette and Nell came across the porch.

"Hi, Zach," Annette said. "Mind if we join you for a while?"

He moved the sandwich wrapping. "Be my guest."

Nell sat on the same step, but at the opposite end. Annette stood at the bottom, stretching her arms and waggling her hands. "Whew, my fingers are cramping from getting every speck of dust up."

She chatted about the schedule remaining before Friday's opening. "Well, I'd better get back in and get started on the windows."

Nell didn't budge.

"Annette," he protested. Steve had made his rules clear.

"It's okay, I'll be right inside."

At least he would stick to Steve's commandment about leaving it up to Nell to talk. They could sit in silence for a month. Fine with him.

"Do you hate Grandmother?" Nell asked abruptly.

Yeah, a month of silence definitely would have been fine with him. But the kid deserved honesty.

"No, I don't hate her." He'd been sure he hated her when he left, but that was a long time ago.

"But you're angry at her."

"She does—she's done things that make me angry, yes."

Nell nodded.

He was starting to hope this line of questioning was over when she spoke again. "Why don't you *like* Grandmother?"

This one he couldn't deny, either.

He thought about the people he liked, those he felt more than liking for. An image of Fran's face, before he'd kissed her last night, formed in his head. That wasn't the liking Nell was asking about.

"With people you like, you usually have things in common. The same things are important to you and you respect the other person. If you don't have that, a lot of times you don't like the person much. That doesn't mean you wouldn't help them if they were in trouble, but they're not someone you want to spend a lot of time with."

"But she's your mother."

"Sometimes that doesn't change things."

Her eyebrows knitted. "I don't know if I like my mother, because she's dead. But sometimes I'm mad at her. She was a bad mother."

He couldn't imagine Steve saying that to a child; Nell must have gotten it from another source. "Why do you say that?"

"I was too little to remember her, but people told me.

Sometimes I just heard." She slanted a look at him, and Zach figured she was checking if he knew she'd heard things last night, too. He let her see that he did. She gave a tiny shrug. "She ran off when I was little, and she took drugs."

"I don't know about all that, Nell. I wasn't here."

"But Grandmother didn't do those things. She's not fun, not like Miss Trudi, but she's not bad. Maybe you should get to know her. Then you wouldn't be so angry at her. Because I don't think you're going to get another mother like I did."

She looked up at the window to Annette, who smiled at her.

"You're lucky, Nell, to have a mother like Annette." He swallowed. "And a father like your dad."

"Yeah," she agreed, as if he'd said she was lucky to live in a world with gravity. "I gotta go. See you later."

Fran closed the dishwasher. Zach flipped off the light, and they started up the stairs. It had been a long day.

The trees were planted. Rob was on his way back to Chicago. Kay was at Miss Trudi's "to keep her company," although she would be back frequently to be with Chester and the puppies. Zach had cooked a pork roast for dinner, and they'd cleaned up together.

And if Fran didn't say something she would explode.

"Zach. I'm sorry." She stopped at the base of the stairs. "You said you'd get the trees to Bliss House safely. I should have trusted you."

"Why should you trust Tobias's bad boy, Fran?"

"Because you're not that boy anymore."

He raised a skeptical eyebrow, but his eyes revealed more complicated reactions.

"I was glad to see you and Steve talking," she said abruptly.

"Yeah, we talked." He gave her yet another look she didn't understand, and gestured for her to go up.

She started climbing the stairs, but obeying his gesture didn't change the fact she was taking control of this conversation.

"That's good. You two need to talk. You can't let this situation drive you apart for good. Have you ever thought about why it bothered you so much when Lana started pushing you as the great Corbett hope?"

"Yeah, I didn't want to be on the front lines taking all her firepower."

She turned at the top of the stairs. "That could be some of it."

He hit her with a blue laser glance that informed her he didn't want to know what the rest of it was. She told him anyway.

"You didn't want to usurp Steve's place. You couldn't stand the idea of being the instrument for displacing or hurting your brother. Maybe that's why you've been so angry at your mother—you felt she was pitting you against Steve."

She'd knocked him off balance. Good. Chewing that thought over might bring him a step closer to reconnecting with Steve. And as long as he was off balance, she might as well get in a few more points.

"I've changed my mind, Zach."

"About?"

"About you being here."

"You think I should leave."

"No. I think you should stay for a different reason."

His shoulders eased. "You'll have to explain that one."

"Your staying can do more than prevent harm to Nell, and by extension Steve and Annette. Your staying can help."

"I have nothing to offer her."

"Yes, you do. First, you can offer her answers. And you can

offer her more love. She has great parents in Steve and Annette, but who says a child should only get a certain amount of love? You can give her something no one else on earth can—your love."

"Ah, Fran."

She wasn't at all sure what that meant. Then he slipped his hand under her hair and around the back of her neck, and she had a pretty good idea.

She'd cupped her hands up in front of her, forming a barrier between their bodies. He stretched across the space and kissed her, light and undemanding.

Then he backed away, his gaze traveling over her face before he bent to kiss her again. Uncertain, she leaned back.

She should say things, explain…

He pursued, taking her mouth.

Her hands uncurled, brushed the open placket of his shirt, closed again. But they couldn't stay still. Not with the way his lips pressed and slid against hers. He angled his head, she answered the movement. Her fingertips touched the underside of his jaw. Then he captured her top lip, sucking on it, and her arms slid around his neck.

He tightened his hold around her, drawing her closer, pressing her breasts against him. He made a sound deep in his throat, a sound he'd made last night, between a growl and hum.

But she forced herself to end the kiss, to break away.

"You don't have to do this, Zach." She touched his cheek.

"Have to?" He looked at her mouth. "Maybe, maybe not. Want to? Oh, yeah."

"But…"

He lifted his head. "Don't you know how beautiful you are? How absolutely amazing? If I'd had condoms with me and any say in the matter, we would have made love last night on the porch."

"Why?"

He half laughed, half groaned. "Why? Because I've wanted you a long time, and last night I got the idea you want me, too."

"A long time? You can't have."

"It's seemed like a long time to me. Probably since you rose out of that lilac bush and gave me hell for not marching up to the front door of Corbett House."

He could have said he'd wanted her since they were kids. Right now she might have believed him. But he wasn't offering the lies Tim had told. He wasn't promising love or forever. He was simply offering this moment.

And she wanted it. She wanted him. She wanted passion.

Calm, reasonable Fran Dalton wanted passion.

She'd tried that once before, but the mistake she'd made then was looking for more than passion. Looking for—and believing—all the promises Tim had made. But Zach made no promises.

So she could accept his passion, couldn't she?

She released a breath she thought she might have been holding all her life. "Yes, I do. I want you."

Taking his hand, she led him into her bedroom. He released her to close the door, so she crossed the expanse of wood floor to the rug beside her bed alone, as she did every night. She stepped out of her shoes and dropped her cardigan on the nearby chair.

But when she turned to see Zach standing by the door, she knew this was not like any other night.

"Are you nervous?" His voice was low.

"Yes."

"So am I." He took a slow step toward her.

"You?"

"You don't think I get nervous?" His next step shrank the space between them to an arm's length.

"No, I don't. Not in situations like this."

One side of his mouth slanted up. He took her hand, kissed the palm, then slid it into the opening of his shirt, then down and to his left, holding it there, trapped between his chest and his hand.

"I've never been in a situation like this before. Because we've never been together before."

His heart beat fast and hard under her hand. More than the rhythm, though, she absorbed the warmth surrounding her hand, surrounding her.

She pushed at his shirt, wanting to see and feel everything. He shrugged out of his clothes with careless grace and impressive speed. Absorbed in exploring him, she barely noticed how he disposed of her clothing…except for the sensations his touch left in its wake. Her breasts felt full and tight, her belly quivering and pulsing.

Lying down on the bed, they kissed. Again and again. She had never realized before that kisses had sounds. The actual sound of their mouths coming together, the inarticulate rumblings from his throat, the moans from hers, the ragged intake of oxygen to fuel the next kiss. Each different.

Face-to-face they kissed and touched and watched.

She licked the hollow at the base of his neck, then lower, to his heart.

He rumbled something and rolled to his back, taking her with him by holding her face between his hands, kissing her eyes, her forehead, her mouth. She backed away, just enough to stroke her hands across his shoulders, then down. He was more beautiful than anything she had ever seen. With her fingers, and then with kisses, she traced the bottom of his rib cage, etched by bone and muscles in perfect proportion, like the arch of a great cathedral.

She kissed lower, and in a motion that sucked the breath from her, he reversed their positions, his weight pressing sensation into her all along her body.

He reached over the edge of the bed and came back with a foil packet. He tore it apart, then adjusted his position to pull on the condom.

Trying to give him more room, she shifted, accidentally scratching a fingernail across his tender skin. He jerked.

She tried to scramble away, but it was impossible with his weight holding her down.

"I'm sorry. I'm sorry. I'm not very good at this—"

"Like hell." He kissed her. Hard. "Any better and I'd need CPR. Besides, it's not you, it's not me. This is us. Together."

He stroked his hand down her thigh, then back up on the inside, the subtlest enticement to make her raise her leg, to open to him. She did, and was rewarded with the sensation of his hips fitting perfectly between her legs and his hard heat nudging against her.

"Ah, Fran."

Slowly, slowly, he slid into her, filling her.

Too slowly.

She made a sound—need, impatience, wanting.

He slid deeper. More. Deeper. There.

"Ohh."

He rose up on his arms, looking into her eyes, a smile pulling his mouth wide. She smiled back, delighted and amazed at this reality, at this rightness.

She flexed her hips, just a bit, just to see… Zach squeezed his eyes shut. She did it again.

"Fran…"

"Now, Zach. Now."

He kissed her as he pulled his hips back, then thrust slowly into her.

She held onto him, felt the tightening and release of his muscles, the cycle coming faster and faster, each withdrawal only a prelude to a deeper thrust.

"Fran…Franny…"

He reached between them, his hand stroking across her, his body thrusting into her.

She held back the sounds, the words welling up in her from somewhere so deep inside she'd never experienced it before. But she couldn't hold back the tremor that came from the same spot. It rocked her, splintered her, left her no solidity or safety in the universe except with this man who shuddered into her, his head thrown back, his lips parted on her name.

"Fran."

Fran looked back from the doorway at Zach sleeping in her bed.

She was glad she hadn't disturbed him; he needed the rest. She'd awakened to find him dreaming, muttering and grimacing, but his body still. Too still. She'd gently pressed her hand to his shoulder and gradually he'd quieted into a normal sleep. Heaven knew how long he'd struggled with the dream before it woke her.

All in all he couldn't have gotten more than a couple hours of real rest, because their sleep had also been disturbed twice in the most amazing ways.

She'd steered away from bad boys all her life, and thought she was so safe with a supposed good guy like Tim. But she hadn't been. So why not take a risk? Especially since there was definitely something to be said for bad boys. They got plenty of practice, so they knew what they were doing.

At least this one did.

Oh, she knew she shouldn't jump to conclusions based on one night. On the other hand, it didn't take more than one sip of champagne to know it wasn't vinegar.

Definitely not vinegar.

Still, her good sense told her that any time she had with Zach was like champagne in another way. The bubbles would go flat in no time now that the bottle was opened. But damn it, she would *not* let herself regret opening that bottle. Having it sitting in the fridge forever would have made it go flat eventually, too. She would have no regrets. None.

Nor would she have any expectations.

Zach had given her an experience unlike any she'd had before.

It wasn't the same for him. Oh, he'd had pleasure—she wasn't that naive. But it was probably no different from what he was used to.

She knew he felt gratitude toward her, and even fondness, and he would never treat her as a commodity the way Tim had.

But she would not mistake integrity, an innate decency and bad-boy technique for anything else.

Zach leaned against the entryway from the hall and surveyed the woman he'd spent the night making love with.

Fran stood at the sink. She wore a cotton shirt under a long, loose sweater, and sweatpants—her anti-sex-appeal uniform.

"Oh!" Turning, she caught sight of him and started, her hands going to her throat. She probably didn't even know it was a self-protective move. "I didn't see you there, Zach.

Good morning. Would you like something for breakfast? Wh-what are you doing?"

Stalking her.

He could tell her that, but words weren't going to cut it. He would just have to batter down those walls of hers again. The woman had crawled out of bed and right into this pretense that nothing had changed. Like what he wanted from her this morning were damned eggs.

He kept closing in on her, walked right through her walls and stood close enough to feel her breath on the skin at the V of his shirt.

With one hand spread wide, he stroked down from her waist and pressed her against him, trapping her between the pressure of his hand and the hardness of his groin.

"Zach, we should talk…"

She didn't push at him or tell him to let her go, as he'd half expected. Instead, she did what the other half of him expected. She arched in an effort to offset the fact that he'd eliminated the space between their lower bodies. All of him welcomed that reaction. The tightness in him twisted harder, her heat compounding his. But he held back the urge to rock, to push against her. Not yet. Not nearly yet.

One flick and the cardigan was open. And what do you know—there was one advantage to these oversize clothes she encased herself in. All it took was a flip on each side and the thing fell off her shoulders and trailed down her arms.

Before she could react, he unbuttoned the flannel shirt one-handed, and with flawless precision, if he said so himself.

"Oh!"

He would have preferred more pleasure in her breathy exclamation, but he could make do with astonishment.

"How did you—?"

"Bad-boy training does come in handy sometimes."

"But…Zach, you shouldn't—"

He never had liked being told what he shouldn't do.

He drew his thumb across her nipple. The tip hardened with pleasure and desire—he knew just how it felt.

"Zach, we can't—"

He didn't like being told what he couldn't do, either.

With one motion, he slid his hand under the bra strap, scooped it over her shoulder and down her arm, then displaced the covering of her bra with his hand.

"The hell we can't," he said into her mouth, just before he plunged his tongue inside in a thrust and retreat, thrust and retreat.

When they were both oxygen-depleted, he trailed his mouth down her throat, over that dip in her collarbone—the same spot she'd licked on him last night, nearly short-circuiting his entire system—then to her breast. He skimmed his teeth gently over her nipple before he took it into his mouth and sucked.

Gasping, she arched, but not to gain space. She rocked against him, panting.

"Franny…?"

It was a question he knew she understood. They wouldn't have to go upstairs, not unless she insisted.

If he could push her now…break through that last shred of her calm. She'd held on to it last night. Despite the surrender of her body to the sensations of lovemaking, he'd felt that ultimate reserve remain.

Footsteps and voices sounded from outside, followed by a brisk knock on the porch door.

Fran gasped. For a second he thought she'd fainted. Instead, she dropped down below the counter level and scooted across the floor toward the door to the formal dining room. From there she could get to the stairway without being seen from the porch.

He was torn between laughing and...oh, hell, not laughing. Because he didn't think he could move. He sure as hell couldn't make the hurried exit she was making.

"C'mon in," he called from behind the protection of the counter.

He heard two voices, an adult and child, on the porch, then the door into the house opened and Kay stuck her head around it. "Nell and I are here to visit Chester and the puppies."

"Fine. I'll go tell Fran you're here in a minute—I need coffee first. Can I bring you some?"

"That would be great."

Upstairs, after taking the time he needed and giving Kay her coffee, Zach leaned against the wall opposite Fran's closed bathroom door.

Fran opened the door. Color surged into her cheeks, and the temptation to scuttle away flickered in her eyes. But she didn't move. "Did I hear Kay and Nell?"

He pushed off the wall, and closed the gap. "Yeah."

"Then we should—"

"Not yet." He slid his hands up under the reinstated cardigan and flannel shirt and rested them at her waist. The tension in her seemed to vibrate through him.

"Zach. We have to go."

"I want you to remember, all day, while you're wearing all these clothes, what it feels like to have my hands under them, touching your skin."

"Can I ask you somethin'?" Nell asked.

"What?"

Thank heavens Kay took the lead in responding. Fran wasn't sure she could get a word out. Her head and way too much of her body remained lost in moments from last night and this morning.

I want you to remember…what it feels like to have my hands…touching your skin.

Zach sat in seeming innocence across from the loveseat she shared with Kay. Damn the man. She could feel the heat and pressure of his touch on every inch of her skin.

"What's it like to have a brother or a sister?" Nell asked.

"I'm no help," Kay said, sounding relieved. "I don't have any."

Nell turned to Fran, then Zach.

Forcing herself to keep her mind off Zach, Fran said, "I've heard that the longest relationship anyone has is with a sibling, so you should take great care of it."

Nell didn't seem impressed, but Fran thought her point had reached its intended target—Zach.

"I think Daddy and Annette are worried I'll feel left out if I had a new baby brother or sister."

Zach was watching a puppy try to clamber over Nell's arm, but Fran thought he recognized the underpinning of her words—faith that Steve, Annette and she were a family, and that was her future.

"Have they said that, Nell?" Kay asked.

"Not exactly. But I know how to make them not worry about it."

"You do?"

She nodded. "First, I'll get one of Chester's puppies and—"

"Wait a minute," Kay protested. "Your dad said you couldn't have one of these puppies. You already have Pansy."

Nell nodded vehemently. "They don't want me to get another puppy because they're afraid Pansy will feel left out. Just like you said." Her gaze pinned Kay.

"I don't remember saying that, and if I did that wasn't what I meant!"

Nell tipped her head to one side. "Well, then why can't I have one of Chester's puppies?"

Kay wrestled with that one for a moment. Then she brightened. "You'll have to ask your parents."

"I will!" Nell bounced up and started out.

"But first you have to go to school," Fran said.

"Only for the morning," Nell called over her shoulder. "Teachers have a planning afternoon."

Kay started dialing her cell phone.

"What are you doing?"

"Calling Annette to warn her that Nell has a new puppy tactic."

That Monday morning Zach had the gardens to himself, which made it easy for his thoughts to wander where they wanted to.

Fran.

He had never had pleasure like he had heating her cool to the boiling point of abandon. To the point, but not past it.

And then she'd tried to wrap her calm back around herself like a cloak.

He picked up the handles of the wheelbarrow and followed the empty path toward the house.

In another of Kay's ideas about how to spread the word on Bliss House, everyone else—including the construction crew—had fanned out in groups of three and four to give presentations about their town's most historic building. They were at the middle schools and high school now, after hitting grade schools in the morning. The younger students were off this afternoon while their teachers prepared for parents' night.

Parents' night.

He'd helped create Nell, but he wasn't her parent.

Could he live with that? Could he live up to Fran's view of him?

Part of him wanted to get out of here. Nell would be better off, secure in having Steve and Annette as her parents. And he wouldn't be torn.

But something…something held him here. Like the old man's grip during those twenty-seven hours whenever he'd had a point to make.

But what was the point?

Zach turned the corner of Bliss House with the wheelbarrow and came face-to-face with Nell.

The hope he read in her face switched to disappointment as she recognized him. He felt a pressure in his chest, as if he couldn't get enough oxygen.

"Oh. It's you."

"Yes. It's me. What's wrong, Nell?"

She looked past him down the path. "I need Fran. Or Max."

"Everybody's doing programs at the schools. What's wrong?"

"Isn't Lenny here? Or Eric? They work with Max. They should be here."

"They're not. Nobody's here but me. Now, what's wrong?"

He saw her weighing the situation. Not wanting to turn to him, but needing… He dropped the wheelbarrow handles and stepped around them. There were no overt signs of injury or illness, but…

"Are you okay? Are you sick or—"

He had one hand on her shoulder, assessing her pupils, breathing, skin color, temperature. All seemed fine. But there were small tears in the long sleeves of her heavy shirt.

"It's not me. It's Pansy." Her voice wobbled.

"Pansies?" He looked at the bright-colored flowers Fran had planted by the front door.

"Not pansies—Pansy. My puppy." The scorn ebbed and fear stepped forward. "She's stuck and she's crying and I can't reach her."

"Stuck where?"

It was as if something unlocked in her, possibly the recognition that he was her only hope. "C'mon, you have to help her."

She fisted her hand around the hem of his T-shirt and yanked. He heard a faint rip when he didn't respond fast enough.

She headed for the farthest, wildest corner of the grounds.

He had a feeling, a bad feeling. They passed the last tree. He could hear the dog's pitiful, low cries, which eased one major concern—it was alive. The sounds came from near the wall. And the only thing between them and the wall were bushes. He'd always liked blueberries. Please…

"There!"

Nell dropped to her knees in the dirt in front of the oldest, biggest, most thorn-laden raspberry canes he'd ever seen. He bent, and through a thicket of crisscrossed canes, he saw a brown-and-white dog not yet out of puppyhood, caught in the V between canes thicker around than his thumbs.

Raspberry bushes.

"Pansy! Pansy!"

The dog moved forward, encountered a thorn, yelped, tried to turn, felt another one and gave a low cry.

"No—don't call her. She needs to stay still. Stay, Pansy."

"She doesn't know that yet," Nell objected.

But apparently the dog recognized what was in her own best interest and stilled.

He straightened.

"Where are you going?" It was less a question than an accusation.

The eyes…the eyes tumbled him back four months. Not the wild eyes of the puppy, but the expectant yet wary eyes of the child, and the wise, resigned yet still expectant eyes of old Miguel.

"I'm looking things over. Talk to her quietly, Nell. Keep her calm."

She talked to the dog, but kept her eyes on him. He tried to ignore her suspicious glare as he assessed the extraction. Leverage could clear part of the path but not all of it. He needed equipment.

See the big picture, focus on the details. Inch at a time.

Zach had relied on those details to give him that little slice of distance from Miguel. It was the only way to keep your heart pumping. Otherwise it could crush you. The death, the sorrow.

Sure, everyone said live rescues weren't the only reward. There was the necessity of finding the dead, for practical reasons like public health and survivors' legal rights, and especially to help the living heal. But live rescues kept you going—either the hope of them or the memory of them.

But with the old man, it was neither.

Everyone had known. Everyone who'd worked like hell to get him out, who'd plotted and strained and sweated and prayed. They'd done their damnedest, even knowing he wasn't going to make it.

Even Miguel. Especially Miguel.

"You can't let Pansy die."

He jerked. He couldn't—wouldn't—promise to hold off death.

"I'll be right back, Nell."

"You're leaving." Mere accusation would have sounded good after those two words. They were a pronouncement of high treason.

"I need to get some things. I'll be right back." He met her eyes. "I'll be right back."

He saw disbelief. He wanted to argue with it, but that would be another moment of pain and fear for the puppy. He wasn't that selfish. Especially when arguing wouldn't convince this child.

He sprinted away.

If he could put his hands on a spreader for a quarter of an hour... He did find loppers, a shovel, three pieces of two-by-four, balancing them along with the tools as he headed back to Nell.

She glared at him.

"You were gone a long time." Her chin wobbled.

Not more than five minutes.

"Your job is to talk to Pansy," he told her. "Let her hear your voice."

The old man had talked. *A lifetime told in twenty-seven hours.*

As Nell talked to Pansy, Zach pulled his gloves on and started cutting with the loppers. The young growth caught on the old canes, his gloves, his shirt, his neck.

He swallowed a curse.

"You don't like raspberries?" Nell's voice quavered.

Pansy wasn't the only one who needed calming. He yanked free of raspberry thorns and kept going. Creating a tunnel to Pansy.

"Not the plants, not since I was a kid."

"Why?"

Inching forward, he told her about picking raspberries as a boy with Steve and Rob by the old highway bridge over Tobias River. She asked question after question. He answered automatically. She'd know details of every outing if he didn't get this dog free soon.

The tunnel wasn't wide enough to accommodate his shoulders as he got in deeper. His shirt and skin took more punishment.

"Got it." He wrapped the end of the leash around his hand. "Call her, Nell."

"Pansy, Pansy, come! Come, Pansy."

But the puppy had learned her lesson from the thorns too well. Moving meant pain, so she held absolutely still, except for trembling.

He had to go in and get her. But, Christ, why did it have to be raspberries? Fate had a wicked sense of humor.

He wedged the two shorter two-by-fours on either side of the tunnel, then put the longer piece between them.

He belly-crawled into the tunnel. Branches curled past the two-by-fours, snagging him. Worse, there were canes under him, tearing at him, piercing his elbow as he used it to pull himself forward.

Another foot.

He looked up, eye to eye with the frightened animal.

"Hi, Pansy," he said softly. "You're going to be a good girl now and come right to me."

He stretched out his gloved hand.

He saw his hand. No longer covered in a rough work glove, but in the latex of his profession. Not moving. Frozen, his hand reaching, not touching. Knowing the old man was dead. Not ready to confirm it.

The puppy whimpered, and he was back in Tobias.

He slipped his hand under Pansy's belly. She spread her stiff legs in classic canine passive resistance, but she was small enough that he drew her to him with no problem. Going backward, the thorns got in a few more jabs.

At last, he cleared the end of the raspberry tunnel and sat back on his haunches, handing the puppy to Nell. It was a reunion of relief and joy, tears and licks.

"She's bleeding!"

Zach shrugged off his torn shirt and wrapped it around the puppy, then handed her back. Nell cuddled the animal.

Car doors closed and voices came from the direction of the drive.

"Zach?" Miss Trudi's voice called.

"In the kitchen garden," he called back. "With Nell."

The tenor of the voices changed, and in seconds, Steve, followed by Annette, then Fran and the rest of them, arrived.

"What happened?" Steve demanded. "Are you okay, Nell?"

"I'm okay, but Pansy…" She held up the wrapped puppy to her father as if he could heal her with his touch.

"Her cuts will need cleaning, but no stitches," Zach said.

"What about yours?" Fran asked.

He looked down at his blood-speckled chest. Some of his, some of Pansy's. "No big deal."

Annette took the puppy from Steve, while he squatted to eye level with Nell.

"How did this happen, Nell?"

"I had Pansy's leash. I was holding it tight, like you said. But then Squid—that's Miss Trudi's cat," she said over her shoulder to Zach before turning back to her parents, "ran along the top of the wall and Pansy—" she flapped one hand "—ski-dabbled."

"Skedaddled," Annette murmured.

"She ran right through the raspberries and she didn't get hurt or anything, but then she turned around and her leash got tangled and I tried to reach her and she tried to reach me and she got stuck. So I went to look for help. But I couldn't find anyone, just him. He cut her out."

Zach helped up the loppers by one handle like a trophy. "The jaws of life."

No one laughed, but the atmosphere did ease, all except around Steve. He didn't look at Zach, only at Nell.

"You and Pansy were supposed to be at Laura Ellen's house, Nell. How did you get here?"

"Her sister drove us. Laura Ellen's got extra homework because she was talking in class."

"Why did you come here? You knew we wouldn't be here. We told you all about it this morning."

Nell said nothing but her gaze slid sideways toward Zach.

Steve stood up abruptly. "We'll talk about this at home. First we'll take Pansy to Dr. Maclaine and make sure she's okay."

Annette touched Steve's arm lightly. But apparently she didn't think that was going to do the trick, because she also turned to Zach, gave him a smile and said, "Thank you, Zach."

"No problem. Glad to help.'

Steve jerked his head in what might have been a nod, but he didn't look at his brother or say more. He picked up Nell, who was still holding the puppy in Zach's shirt, and strode toward the cars.

Annette patted Zach's arm, exchanged a look with Fran, then followed.

Zach watched the three of them—four including the dog—a family, united by a hundred, maybe a thousand such crises overcome. By a thousand moments of love and connection.

He had just this one with the child he'd helped create.

"C'mon, Zach," Fran said from beside him. "Let's get you cleaned up. Looks like you've been shot with buckshot."

"A thousand cuts," he reminded her.

A thousand cuts. A thousand connections. That was the difference.

"Here's the first-aid kit. Now, you sit down and let me fix you up." Fran steered him by the arm toward the closed toilet seat.

She'd fussed about his scratches in her understated way, and couldn't be budged from her insistence that they return to her house to tend them.

It was time to tell her. After last night, past time.

But he didn't have to tell it all.

"I'll do it, Fran. This is my job." He took the first-aid kit from her, put it on the edge of the sink.

"You don't have to be macho or—"

"I'm not being macho. I mean it literally. This is my job."

He reversed places with her and urged her to sit while he perched on the side of the tub. Her head came up, her eyes wide. But she said nothing.

"You might even say it's my calling." His mouth twisted a bit—not at the idea of having a calling, but at the irony that Zach Corbett had ended up with one.

"You don't work for the county government? You lied to me?"

"I didn't lie about anything I told you—I do work for the

county. But I didn't tell you everything. I trained in the army as a medic."

"A medic?" The blankness sharpened to recognition in an instant. "That's why you *knew* what to do for Muriel when she fainted."

"That's because it is what I do. I work for Fairfax County, Virginia, now with the fire-and-rescue department."

"But why didn't you tell me?"

"There's more. I'm a member of Virginia Task Force One—it's an elite urban search-and-rescue team. We work here in the States and we're one of two in the country that the feds can deploy overseas. It's…it's the best thing I've ever been involved with, Fran."

Her mouth worked a moment before sound came out.

"What do you do?"

"Me? I'm a small cog. But the task force—we respond to disasters, from hurricanes to earthquakes to bombings of buildings. We were in Turkey and Iran, and then the big one last spring in South America."

"The Americans who rescued that family that came out alive after four days—I saw that on TV. And—" Her mouth formed an O. "That's why the reporter who came after Kay knew you. He recognized you. But…I would have recognized you. If you'd been one of the rescuers they showed on TV, I would have recognized you. Even if you used a different name."

"That was Blue Team's rescue. I was on Red Team."

Their extraction had been news for only a blink of the eye, before Blue Team's rescue had drawn all the attention.

"But…why haven't you said anything? Why haven't you told your family? Oh. Or maybe you did and…"

"You're the first one I've told, Fran. Kay figured it out, thanks to that tabloid sleaze, but she agreed it was my choice whether to tell or not. As for why…I don't know if I can explain. That's who I am now, but coming back here, back to Tobias, I'm still the kid who ran away. I didn't want… I couldn't…"

She put one hand over his, brushed back his hair with the other.

"They'd be so proud of you. As proud as your friend Elliott must have been."

Training kept his muscles still when they wanted to jerk. But nothing could make him talk about whether Elliott had been proud of him.

"I'm not interested in buying the Corbetts' approval. That's not why I do it."

"I know, and that's why it wouldn't be buying approval."

"They're comfortable seeing me a certain way. Why shake them up?"

"Because you're not twenty anymore, Zach. Whether they accept you as the man you are now or not, you have a responsibility to show them that man. That hero."

"I'm not—"

"A hero," she repeated firmly. "I promise not to tell anyone else, but I will not pretend you're not one. How did you come to be on the task force, Zach?"

It all came out as he treated his cuts. Training in the army, joining a smaller search-and-rescue team, moving to Virginia to join the Fairfax department as a paramedic, then working for more than a solid year at getting on the task force roster and waiting another year before his first deployment.

He told her about the training, about the characters, about that first deployment. He made her laugh, he made her mouth form that tempting O again, he made her eyes widen and tear up.

Letting her see how much the work, the team, and the team members meant to him, he told her everything.

Except about his last deployment.

Chapter Ten

"What's wrong, Fran?"

"Nothing. Just need to get to work. I have phone calls to make."

"I'll go out and get something to put together for dinner."

"Please don't do that. We have so many leftovers from the weekend. We need to clean out the refrigerator."

"Okay. I'm going for a run, unless…you're sure nothing's wrong."

"Not a thing. Enjoy your run."

The door closed behind Zach and she sat at the table, the two calls on her list already completed. She'd lied to have an excuse not to talk to him.

Wrong? How could there be anything wrong?

Zach Corbett had found his calling. He helped people. He saved their lives. He closed the gaping unknown for survivors of tragedies searching for their loved ones. He was a hero.

No, not just a hero. A rescuer.

She laughed. Startled at the sound, she swallowed it. Zach Corbett was a rescuer. He didn't need help, he gave it. He was no longer the boy with angry blue eyes, the swagger and the dark confusion swirling around him. He was sure and grounded—she'd sensed that in him the first day. She'd told Steve that.

And yet she'd indulged in some idiotic fantasy, thinking she was rescuing him.

He hadn't been so...*attentive* yesterday out of gratitude that she'd listened to him, perhaps given him a bit of guidance. She'd been fooling herself.

But, wait... He *had* touched her and held her like...like a man who wanted a woman.

If it wasn't in gratitude for helping him, then why...?

Don't you know how beautiful you are? How absolutely amazing?

Oh, God. Oh, God. He'd been rescuing *her*.

"Zach."

Steve swung up onto the bleachers beside him.

Zach was surprised and not surprised. He'd migrated to his old spot in the bleachers without conscious thought. Far left end, third row from the top. Gave a good view of the practice field without being as visible as you would be on the top rows or down lower.

"Steve."

"Fran said you went for a run. I thought I might find you here. We need to talk."

"Yeah, we do."

Their silence announced that neither knew where to start.

"I love football," Zach finally said. "I used to sit here

watching practice. Day after day. Drills, conditioning, all the boring crap. Every minute. I could probably still run a practice from heart."

"You wanted to play that badly."

They'd both played sports as youngsters. Then Ambrose Corbett had died, and Lana had refused to let Steve play basketball or Zach play football. Only the country-club sports—golf, tennis and swimming—would do for her sons. Steve had shifted to swimming. Zach had refused any sport.

"Yeah. I wanted to play that badly."

"I didn't know. I thought…"

"You thought I didn't give a shit about anything." Steve started to make a gesture. Zach cut it off. "It wasn't your fault. I made sure nobody knew I wanted it, that I wanted anything."

Steve glanced at the field. "You never told me how you felt about football because you thought I sold out by settling for swimming."

Zach twisted his neck around so fast it cracked. "Hell, no!"

"I wondered if seeing what happened when I wanted things made you think it was better to not want anything," Steve said. "That spring, after Mother realized I wasn't going to change my mind about marrying Annette…I know it made things harder on you."

"It's a game I've played with myself sometimes, wondering how long I would have lasted in your shoes growing up. Because you were the real rebel."

"Me?" Steve laughed. "You're the one who rode the motorcycle, had long hair, raised hell and left town. I was the one who made every curfew, never talked back and settled back here. Ask anybody in town and they'll tell you—Zach Corbett's the rebel."

"And they'd all be wrong. You were the real rebel because

you had the strength to be independent. I ran because I don't—didn't—have that strength. You didn't have to talk back to her because you did what you knew was right for you. You could come back because you would keep living your way wherever you were."

The amusement had died from Steve's eyes. "And you couldn't?"

"No. If I'd stayed I would have caved in."

"You weren't caving in. I heard you—"

"Words—yeah, I had words. They weren't going to be enough, not against her strength of will. When she gets that look…"

"Like she's been dipped in a vat of instant lacquer."

"That's the one." Zach's grin twisted in the middle. "That offended-with-the-worm-that-is-my-son look."

Steve shook his head, thoughtful. "I think it's when emotions threaten. She doesn't know how to deal with them. So she puts on that iron facade."

"That's no facade, that's Lana through and through. I'll give her this—the woman has always known what she wanted. And I didn't. All I had was knowing I didn't want to do it her way."

He gestured toward the field.

"That's the difference between us, Steve. You were like the kids playing offense—always heading toward something, a certain kind of life. That's what kept pushing you forward no matter how many obstacles she put in your way. She knew that, too. That's why Lana didn't fight you harder over marrying Annette. You were fighting for something. Me, I was just fighting *against*. All my life, fighting *against*. All defense."

He was still watching the players, so he felt more than saw Steve's frown. Zach never had been much for explaining. But something pushed him to want to explain now.

Truth and oil always come to the surface. He could hear the old man saying that.

"See number forty-two, the running back? Watch how he moves through this play—he's running to get someplace. There—see him? Even when he gets tackled, his legs are still going, trying to go forward. Now watch somebody on defense—number sixty-three."

The ball was snapped and the players surged into motion. The lineman he'd arbitrarily picked pushed up against an opposing lineman, his big legs driving hard. Then the offensive player he was matched against hitched a step and slid to one side. Number sixty-three, abruptly denied an opposing force, lurched three strides then tumbled down without anyone touching him.

"That was me, Steve. Number sixty-three. Fighting my damnedest when something stood in front of me, and falling over when I didn't have something to fight against."

Steve stared at the field while the players went through two plays. "That's why you left. You had that all figured out and—"

Zach interrupted with a harsh laugh. "Hell, no, I didn't have it figured out. I didn't have a damned thing figured out. I just knew I had to get away. Some thread of self-preservation. It wasn't more than a couple weeks before I realized that without Lana Corbett to go against, I didn't have anything holding me up."

He swore. "Once I convinced myself I had to come back. Somebody had to fight her and maybe that's what I was meant to do. I reached the town sign. It was dead dark, and the mist swirled in from the lake and made the lights go soft like maybe they didn't exist. Like—what's the movie, the one with the town that disappears?"

"Brigadoon."

"Yeah, like Brigadoon. The town disappeared. So I turned my bike around and rode away."

"Did you think about Lily?"

"Are you asking if I knew she was pregnant when I left?"

"No." The word sounded raw. "I know you better than that, Zach. I'm asking if you still had feelings for her."

Zach shook his head. "I broke it off in February. The last time Lily and I had sex was the end of January, beginning of February."

"But I saw you… I saw the two of you coming out of the motel. That was spring. And that night at home, you said—"

"I remember. You tried to tell me to watch out for Lily. And I said it was too late. It was. Because it was over. She'd been trying to get me in bed that afternoon. I said no—at least I had that much integrity. When you saw us at the motel, we were coming out and I was telling her she'd find somebody better."

"That means Nell—"

"Must have been conceived the last time we were together."

The silence that fell between them allowed sounds from the field to well up. Shouted signals, grunts, thuds, coaches' words of praise or correction. But Zach also thought he could hear Steve's thoughts.

"Lana's wrong about Lily sleeping with anybody else," Zach said.

Steve turned to him, and waited.

Zach told him that Lily wouldn't have risked not having a Corbett baby, and Steve nodded. Then he said, "It doesn't make any difference who Nell's biological father is. I'm her father now."

He waited, as if he expected Zach might argue. Then Steve added, low and even, "Zach, you've got to let her go."

"I don't know if I can."

* * *

"Fran." Even over the sound of the shower she heard Zach's voice clearly. As clearly as if he weren't outside the bathroom door.

Had Steve found him? Maybe he wanted to talk.

"I'm in the shower, Zach."

"I know. Why is the light off?"

Oh, God, he wasn't on the other side of the door, he was on *this* side of the door.

With a firm grip on the shower curtain, she stuck her head out of the gap between it and the tile wall.

"Zach, what are you doing in here? You have to get out."

"Why?"

"Because—because I don't want you in my bathroom when I'm taking a shower."

"You do remember we made love last night?"

Remember? She'd felt the tightening at the pit of her belly all day.

"Besides," he said. "I can't see anything in here. It's dark."

Not dark enough that she couldn't see him taking his clothes off. He was beautiful, so beautiful. And then he was in the shower with her, tugging the curtain from her hold, then finding other places to put his hands. Warm, smooth places that responded and swelled.

"Zach, what are you doing?"

"The old line is that if you don't know what I'm doing, I'm not doing it right. But you do know. So I am doing it right."

And he was. Oh, he was.

"Stop. You have to stop."

He released her immediately. "What is it, Fran? What's wrong?"

"I…what happened last night was wonderful, and I appre-

ciate it more than I can tell you. I'd forgotten—no, I never knew
I could feel like that. It was kind of you to teach me—"

"*Kind? Teach you?* I was not conducting a damned sex
workshop."

"I'm thanking you."

"Could have fooled me."

"I'm trying to tell you that I understand."

"Do you? Then explain it to me."

"I know you've been grateful for my concern about the situation with Nell. And you might see a woman like me and
think I'm lonely or—"

"Is that what you think? I saw poor lonely Fran, no one to
love, no one loving her, and I felt sorry for you? Pity and gratitude as an aphrodisiac? Is that what you think?"

She winced at his sharp tone. "That's not—"

"Damn right it's not. You've held out on me, Fran. That
isn't calm you have, it's insulation to keep other people from
getting too close." Without touching her, he came almost nose
to nose, the heat from his body and his anger reaching her in
waves. "Tell me. Who told you you were any particular kind
of woman? Was it the guy in Madison after you graduated?"

She gaped at him. "How do you know about Tim?"

Now he looked grim. "Tim, huh. So what did this jackass
do?"

"Zach, the hot water's running out. Let me finish my
shower—alone—and we can talk later."

"We're talking now." He reached past her and turned off
the water. Then he opened the curtain enough to grab her bath
sheet from the rack. "What happened with Tim?"

She wrapped the bath sheet around her, hands crossed over
where one end tucked in, but tried once again. "Zach—"

"Talk."

So she did. A quick, unemotional and tactfully expurgated accounting of her doomed romance. She tried not to look at Zach, but quickly discovered that standing face-to-face with a man in a bathtub didn't leave much else to look at. Especially not when the one time she looked down made her forget what she was saying entirely, and Zach had to prompt her about how Tim had seemed so gentlemanly and undemanding.

When she finished he was quiet.

Then he shook his head. "For a woman so smart about other people, you don't have a clue about yourself. Not a clue. You believed this jackass? Took his word for who you are?

"Fran, when we were kids, you scared the hell out of me. You were quiet and contained and you never fell for my bull. And when I came back and saw you standing up in the middle of that patch of garden, with leaves in your hair and those ridiculous clothes you wear to try to hide that body, I knew I'd been right to be scared of you. You are one dangerous woman. You go to my head like 400-proof whiskey. And you go to my body like…" He took one of her hands and placed it on his chest. "I don't think I have to explain after last night."

Even if she'd known what to say, she couldn't have mastered language at that instant.

"I want to kiss you, Fran. Is that okay?"

She nodded.

Their only contact was her hand on his chest, but she felt the power of him all around her.

His mouth touched hers lightly. Separated, and returned. She parted her lips, but he didn't enter her mouth. He kissed the center of her bottom lip, the right side of her top lip, and every other portion, pressing gently or strongly, sucking into his mouth, or whispering across.

Fran slid her hand up his chest, over his shoulder and

around his neck, drawing him down to her, stroking her tongue deep inside his mouth.

"Fran, Fran." He rested his forehead against her. "I want to make love to you. But the protection's in the other room. And you still have shampoo in your hair. So we'll take it slow."

He loosened the bath sheet from her and tossed it over the rod, giving her a look that did not make her want to go slow. And then he reached around her again, rubbing and sliding against her bare, cooled skin with his bare, heated skin. When the warm water came on, it couldn't compete.

He massaged the shampoo out of her hair, then extended the massage, kneading her scalp, turning her so her back was to him, working down her neck, across her shoulders, down her arms.

"Do you take showers in the dark a lot?"

Enough light filtered in that it wasn't totally dark, but she was too limp to argue. "Uh-huh."

"Hmm."

"Hmm, what?"

"I like it." He leaned closer, so his next words were a warm breath at her ear. "But I think I'd like your bed better right now."

She turned, put her arms around his neck and said "Yes" against his mouth.

They made love. Slow and aching, yet soothing the ache.

And then it wasn't slow at all, the tremors coming so hard that Fran couldn't hold them or the sounds back. She didn't want to. She surrendered her calm, her insulation to Zach willingly.

She held back only one thing, one word.

Fran dozed afterward, her cheek on Zach's chest. Amazing how comfortable a pillow something so hard could be. When she woke, she knew he was awake.

He told her about his talk with Steve. He didn't need to tell her he didn't know what he would do about Nell.

She led him into more talk about his work as an EMT and with the task force. In his answers to her questions, she heard the sureness, the groundedness she'd sensed in him that first day. He was a man doing what he was meant to do.

"How do you deal with it, Zach, being closed in, digging through ruins, crumbling buildings hanging over you? How do you deal with the fear and the stress?"

"The stress doesn't usually hit until after, sort of a delayed reaction." He shifted, putting his arm over his eyes, shadowing his face. "Fear doesn't factor in. That's what training's for—how to do the job and how to know which jobs you can't do. You can't put yourself into many situations where you're in danger before the team kicks you out—because that makes more work for everyone.

"But being closed in? Now that's bad. A lot of times you get in areas where the air's been trapped and it's stale and sour and foul and…" His eyes dimmed as his voice trailed off. She could imagine what could contribute to the air being so foul. Yes, she could imagine it, but he *knew* it.

"You don't like being closed in? Then how on earth can you do that job?"

"Because the people who might be trapped don't like it any better than I do, and we're their best hope." He said it as if it were obvious. Simple.

"Besides," he added, "there's that amazing feeling of coming out. That instant you step into the open, and there's only space around you and you can taste the fresh air. It's like walking out of a tomb."

She suppressed a shiver at the phrase, not wanting to interrupt his concentration.

"Sometimes I think that's the reason I do it. To get that feeling. It wouldn't feel that good if it didn't feel so bad before."

What a rush of freedom he must have felt when he'd left Tobias, Fran thought, for surely he'd had that sense of being trapped here, even entombed. He'd broken free and he'd been able to breathe.

"Wait a minute. You go into bombed buildings and work in earthquake zones where they're still having aftershocks and—"

"It's not that bad, Fran. We take every precaution and safety's always the first priority."

"—and you're afraid of *raspberry* bushes?"

She saw the glint in his eyes a split second before he twisted, pinning her below him. "I told you, not afraid. Just a healthy respect."

"I don't know why your stubborn brother's insisting on this stupid prenup," Kay groused. "We should be going over there to work with all of you."

Kay, Annette and Nell had shown up this morning for another before-school visit to Chester and the puppies. Each day the puppies grew more independent and Chester less protective. Now the dog rested her head on Kay's knees and kept only one eye on the six fur balls climbing around Nell.

Zach was putting new laces on a pair of high-top leather shoes.

"Couldn't you do the prenup later?" Annette asked.

"Rob says we have to give the guy time to work on it so it's done well before the wedding."

"Have you decided on a wedding date?"

Kay grinned widely. "What do you think of a Christmas wedding?"

"I think you're nuts. A wedding in December? In Wisconsin? And at Christmastime? You know the risk that nobody'll be able to get here? Or they'll never be able to leave."

"I know. But I don't want to wait. If we could pull it off for Thanksgiving…but Rob's not sure he'll be done in Chicago in time and Dora won't be back from France until early December."

"What about your parents?" Fran asked.

"They won't be coming to the wedding. They'll come to Chicago, but they refuse to venture to Tobias. Mother shuddered at the idea."

"Then maybe Tobias isn't—"

"Oh, yes, it is. We're getting married in Tobias."

Fran laughed. "I think you're nuts, but okay."

Kay turned to him. "And you'll promise to come back for the wedding, right, Zach?"

He hadn't let himself think beyond the present. Now, a vision of the Dalton house decorated for Christmas and Fran with snowflakes in her hair grabbed at him.

He fought off the image. "I doubt I'll have any leave left at that point."

"But—"

"Fran, I'm going to head over to Bliss House, check the stakes on the saplings."

Annette looked at her watch. "Yikes, look at the time. We'd all better get over there—did I tell you the news? Lana's volunteered to help. Can you believe it? Nell, you better get started to school now. And Kay, do you have that book on dog training you said I could borrow? We've got to keep Pansy from running away. No more raspberry patches, right, Nell?"

"I'll get the book," Kay said.

Fran stood, too. "Zach, if you'll wait a few minutes, I'll go with you. I have to put some laundry in."

He was already at the door. "Take your time. Come along later."

"But…"

He left her protest behind him, but Zach heard steps following him. Before he'd covered half the distance to his car, Nell caught up with him walking her bike.

"Can I ask you somethin'?"

He glanced toward the porch where the three women now stood, looking toward them. They'd probably be wondering what this was about, since they wouldn't be able to hear from there. "Okay."

"Were you and my daddy ever good brothers?"

He looked down at the intense blue eyes studying him. "Yes."

"When you were picking raspberries?"

"Yeah, and a lot of other times. Steve was a good older brother."

"Were you a good younger brother?"

He gave a half grunt, half chuckle. "I was a pain in the— I was a pain."

She appeared to contemplate that. He thought the questioning might be over. No such luck.

"Did you want to marry my—Lily?"

"No."

"Did you love her?"

"No."

She pinned him with her solemn stare. After what seemed a week, she gave a small nod, as if he'd passed some test.

"I cared about her, and enjoyed being with her. She had a lot of good qualities."

"Like what?"

"Determination." That one came quickly, perhaps because he saw it in Lily's daughter. Was there anything else of Lily in Nell? Anything he could tell this child? "She liked animals. And people. And she liked to have fun."

"Can I ask you somethin' else?"

"Okay." This one had to be easier.

"Do you love Fran?"

Oh, hell.

Chapter Eleven

"She said she'd come, but I didn't believe it," Annette muttered.

Fran, Annette and Suz sat on the front steps of Bliss House, synchronizing their lists and schedules for the final countdown to the opening. They had looked up to see Lana Corbett coming down the walkway toward them. She wore a short wool jacket and matching skirt in marine blue, hose, low heels and pearls.

Fran felt a momentary regret that she hadn't found time to look at Kay's clothes, before she reminded herself that her pullover and loose jeans were practical for a day working around the gardens.

"Hello, Lana," Annette said with a genuine smile. "We're so glad you could come."

Lana inclined her head regally. "What is it you want me to do?"

"Volunteers are making decorations and—"

"I don't have any skill at that." Lana looked almost alarmed.

"That's okay. They're getting the programs ready for the opening, too. Your help will be greatly appreciated."

"Very well." She started to follow the walkway around the house, then stopped. "Annette, there is something I hoped to make clear…"

When Lana's stiff voice trailed off, Fran felt as if she were holding her breath. She sensed the older woman faced a hurdle she was not at all certain she could clear.

"Yes, Lana?" Annette asked in an encouraging tone.

"I want you and Steve and…" She glanced at Fran, then looked back to Annette. "That day at your house, when I suggested a DNA test, it was to prove Nell's a Corbett, not to disprove it. When she gets older, there could be rumors, stories… Nell might suffer."

And in that instant Fran saw that Lana was a woman who cared. Who cared very much. Often about the wrong things, or in the wrong way, yet cared deeply. And didn't know how to reach out, how to give love to those she cared about.

She didn't even know how to talk to them. She had given this message to Annette to carry to Steve and, Fran supposed, to her for Zach.

"Thank you for telling me, Lana. I appreciate your concern for Nell."

"Yes, well, she is my granddaughter."

She walked away then, clothes perfect, hair perfect, posture perfect.

The three younger women sat in silence well after she was gone.

"She's not what we all think she is, is she?" Suz said at last.

Annette released a long, slow sigh. "It's more complicated

than that. She *is* what everyone thinks she is, but she's also more. Back in the spring, when Steve and I got together and she was trying to get Miss Trudi put in a home and to take over Bliss House, I had this moment…I saw her…" She shook her head. "I knew she was lonely. I could see that so clearly, and I felt sorry for her at the same time I was so angry at her for doing these things to Miss Trudi."

"Not to mention how she tried to come between you and Steve," Suz said.

Annette flashed a grin. "Right, no need to mention that, since I won that war. But seriously, I think she's incredibly lonely, and she makes me so sad."

"So you're behind Nell spending time with her?" Fran asked.

"Oh, Steve's the one who…"

Fran let her see her disbelief and Annette's protest wound down. "Yes. I've encouraged that."

"I wondered. It didn't seem in keeping with the way he's always handled his mother."

"What do you mean?"

"Steve sidestepped Lana, simply ignored her or sometimes froze her out of his life. So deliberately encouraging Nell to have contact with her didn't fit. His style's to disconnect from her."

Annette nodded slowly. "You're right. What about Zach?"

"Oh, Zach always squared off with her, standing in her face, shouting his defiance. Taking the battle right to her."

"Then why did he run away?"

"Because he was afraid he was losing." Fran stared at a small, brave rose blooming in a shaft of fall sunlight. "And at the same time he was afraid he'd win by defying her in a way that would break her for good. He couldn't do that, because she's his mother, and deep down he loves her."

* * *

Do you love Fran?

Nell, that's one question I'm not answering. That's not any of your business.

Nell had considered him for an instant, then said *Okay*, got on her bike, waved and was gone.

Zach wished the echo of her question was as easy to send on its way. *Do you love Fran?*

What the hell could he give her? That was a better question.

The answer had him in a foul mood that got worse when he walked into Bliss House near noon and found Lana among the volunteers in the tearoom folding programs for the opening.

He returned her look coolly, then went to the far side of the room for a soft drink, joining Max and Suz by the cooler.

"When are Kay and Rob coming?" Miss Trudi asked. She was folding programs at the same table with Lana.

"Not for a while," Fran said. Her fingers never slowed in making an elaborate bow for the basket that would hold the seed packets. "They're meeting with a lawyer about a prenup."

"It's sensible of Rob to protect his assets," Lana said.

Zach snorted. "Kay's family's the one with the bucks—"

"Don't be vulgar, Zachary."

He thought better of responding with something truly vulgar and simply finished his thought. "Rob's the one who wants to make sure it's ironclad that he gets none of her money."

"I know how he feels," Max murmured as he stacked folded programs into a box.

Suz made a face at him. "After they're married, Rob will figure out what's hers is his and vice versa. *He'll* probably figure it out fast."

Max smiled at her.

"Yeah, but in this case," Zach said, "Kay doesn't want the

money, either. It's going to be the only prenup that's ironclad that neither one gets anything."

"Absolute foolishness," Lana said.

An awkward silence fell at that proclamation.

"The only person I've known who'd agree with that position, Lana," Zach said, "was Lily."

"Don't speak to me of Lily."

"You must have seen the irony in the situation, Lana. Lily—the one from the right family, the one you wanted for Steve because she was *appropriate* for a Corbett—turning out to be—"

"She deceived all of us."

"Not Steve. He had her figured out in high school. And I can't say she deceived me. I knew she really wanted Steve, because he was the Corbett heir. I was a runner-up prize."

"There is no need to be vulgar. I was mistaken in her," Lana said coldly.

"Maybe. Or maybe you recognized a kindred spirit."

"That's nonsense."

"She was pregnant by a guy who took off, but she landed on her feet by latching on to a Corbett who came to the rescue."

Lana had gone white, her lipsticked mouth standing out against her paleness. "I did not latch on to your father. He loved me. And he loved Steven. But you—"

"Yeah, I know, I was a constant disappointment."

She rose, aligned a stack of unfolded programs.

"You refused to give his name and his heritage the respect he deserved, and yet he loved you. More than you ever saw. More than he loved me."

She walked out, her heels clicking on the wood floor. The same sound as on the porch the day he'd left, but slower.

Zach took another soft drink, ignoring the looks zinging around, especially Fran's. But he'd still seen the mix of concern and exasperation in her face.

Into the silence, Miss Trudi said, "You might as well have called your mother a gold digger, Zach."

He opened his mouth to say *Damn straight*. But Miss Trudi beat him to the punch.

"As your grandparents did." She nodded, looking around the room. "I believe it is time to tell you about when Lana came to Tobias. She was carrying you, Steve. She was pregnant with you before she embarked on a whirlwind courtship with Ambrose."

"How long have you known?" Steve asked.

"From the beginning."

"Why didn't you ever tell me?"

"It wasn't anybody's place to tell you except Lana's or Ambrose's. I tried to nudge him. He said he loved you and that was all that mattered. You remember that stiff way he had when he felt strongly about something.

"As for your mother, she reacted with flat denial. As if I hadn't heard the family talking when Ambrose first brought her here. You know he was past fifty, and she was—well, she never admitted to being as young then as she probably was, as she won't admit to being as old now as she is.

"Ambrose's parents raised a mighty fuss—in their own way. Quiet and stern and bristling with rectitude. Ambrose said they were married, and that was that. They gave Lana a hard time, especially Aunt Joan. She'd prune up at any mistake Lana made—grammar, forks, talking too loudly, the wrong clothes. I thought Lana might explode those first months. Especially because Aunt Joan and Uncle Herbert laid down the law and basically said she couldn't go out of the house while she was pregnant—*expecting* as they said.

"You came along, Steve, and she was a new mother with a colicky baby, and frequently not in any state for socializing. Lana had been placed on her first board—the hospital auxiliary, Aunt Joan's private fiefdom—when she became pregnant with Zach and returned to seclusion. Uncle Herbert died the month before Zach was born, Aunt Joan three months after. Aunt Joan's funeral was the true coming out of Lana Corbett. It was astonishing to realize that she not only had learned all the lessons they'd taught her, but had become more Corbett than the Corbetts."

"So, she wasn't welcomed with open arms by her in-laws," Zach said. "That doesn't excuse her."

"Ah, Zach, you are far too hard on your mother. You always have been."

He'd heard about some of his mother's machinations against Miss Trudi, and against Steve and Annette's reconciliation. "You never had any time for Lana, either, Miss Trudi."

"Things change. And your mother has been trying these past months. I truly believe she is trying to change."

"Not Lana Corbett. She won't ever change."

"Why not? You did. And you are your mother's son."

Zach picked up his shoes, planning to put them on in the hall. "Zach?"

Fran's slow, warm voice almost pulled him back to the bed. But she hadn't gotten much rest last night, and with the opening ahead of her later today, she'd be worn out. "It's okay, Fran, go back to sleep."

But she sat up. "Where are you going?"

"To run."

"Now? It's dark."

"It's okay," he repeated.

"Why, Zach? Why do you run in the middle of the night?" She cut off his search for a plausible explanation. "You had a dream. Another dream."

"How did you know…?" Probably the same way Waco did. "I didn't mean to wake you."

"Zach." She stretched a hand. Too far away to touch, yet it tugged at him. "Tell me."

He could have told Taz, he'd have understood. He should have told Doc, it was what he was there for. He would have told Waco, if he'd had the words then.

Now he did. Where they came from he didn't know. He'd think about that later, why they came now, with this woman, and hadn't with the men he had shared so many experiences with, counted as friends, trusted.

"Our last deployment, four months ago." He stood at the end of her bed, resting his hands on top of the smooth edge of the footboard. "It was a textbook earthquake search. The dog alerted, structural checked it over and said we could work it. The tech-search guys homed right in on the subject, and then the rock breakers got started. One layer at a time. Careful. It was a bad spot. A lot of pancaking. After a couple of layers, Doc and I could get in, at least enough to see him, to reach his head and upper torso. But from his waist down…"

He paced to the window, then turned to say these words to her face.

"He couldn't survive his injuries. Even if we could get him out without killing him right then, he'd die soon. And the team couldn't get him out. I could see it in their faces after the first couple of layers. They kept working. But each layer they took off, each assessment made it clearer. They couldn't extricate him and we couldn't keep him alive." He cleared his throat.

"Victims die. It happens. We all know it. It's a given in what we do. I've had patients die before, and this wasn't a kid or…"

"But this victim dying bothered you. Leaving him hurt you."

He shook his head. "We don't leave them, not once we've found them. We don't just say, see ya, be back when we can. Somebody stays with the patient, keeps the IV going, does what he can. The only time we leave them is if higher command says we've gotta get out because something's too dangerous for us to stay, tremors or explosions or something. Because if we get hurt or killed, nobody gets helped. As soon as it's over, we're back in. And the whole team's working: delayering debris, planning the evacuation when the patient's free, preparing an amputation if we have to extricate."

"Not even amputation…?"

He shook his head. "He was pinned across the middle. But what was pinning him also held him together." He pulled in a breath. "The team keeps trying, keeps working, keeps scrambling for a solution. And my job is to control the pain, keep him calm. I've done it before. It's not what you hope for. You want to fight to save people. Just sitting back and listening is… But if you can ease it some…"

He looked up at her, hoping she understood. She did. He saw in her face that she'd experienced it with her mother and father. You helped them to keep living until they died, and that made it bearable.

"But this man was different," she said gently. Yes, she understood.

"Yeah. He was."

"What was he like, Zach?" She reached for him again, this time taking his hand. She urged him to sit, and he did.

"He was about seventy. His name was Miguel, and he

talked all the time. English, Spanish, back and forth. He had a saying for everything."

He told her about Miguel's account of his life, how he had left a wife and children in his native village and moved to the city and created an entirely new life, and how the new life eventually fell apart. His second wife had left him. He was estranged from his now-grown children. He was alone.

"He asked me about my life," Zach said. "Wouldn't be put off. Wanted to hear all about my family and growing up. When I told him I'd left here and hadn't been back in eight years, he said I was making the same mistake he had. That I should learn from him, that if you build a new house on the foundation of an old one without clearing all the rubble, the new one will soon crash down around you."

He waited, but she made no judgments, drew no parallels, she simply listened.

"You asked me why I came back to Tobias, Fran. Miguel—he's the reason. I keep dreaming about him. About his life, about what he said. I can't shake it. I got sent to Doc—he'd been there, too, and he figured it had to do with Miguel, that Miguel had connected with me and that made it personal. But I couldn't…I didn't tell him much. So he said to take some time off, get my head straight." He twisted a grin. "It was not a suggestion, it was an order. Then I had to figure out what the hell to do with the time off. And I couldn't stop thinking of something Miguel said."

The past will not stop speaking to me until I answer it.

He'd said that several times in the hours they talked, especially when he spoke about leaving his first family. But this time Miguel had grabbed his arm, digging into Zach's flesh with surprising strength, his black eyes burning with the knowledge of his own death and with a message. This time he turned the words on Zach.

The past will not stop speaking to you until you answer it.

That was when the dream always woke him, the feel of that grip on his arm, the words in his head.

"He told me, *The past will not stop speaking to you until you answer it.* I came back to Tobias to answer the past so it would stop speaking to me."

Fran supposed she should have expected it. With so many citizens of Tobias packed into and around Bliss House for the three days of the opening weekend, the gossip mills were bound to kick into overdrive.

Saturday afternoon, she found Zach collecting the trash from a full bin along one of the paths.

He'd withdrawn since telling her about Miguel, the man he hadn't been able to save.

She hadn't lectured him about realizing he couldn't save everyone—he knew that. But knowing wasn't enough. Believing it had to be.

And she couldn't help but wonder if there was a connection, not only to the death of his mentor Elliott earlier this year, but further back to his father. A father who had died around the same age Elliott and Miguel had, yet before Zach could know him well.

A woman's voice floated from the Moonlight Garden on the other side of a hedge.

"I always said Zach Corbett's not the kind you could rely on. Wild, that's what he was—and is!"

Another voice said, "But are you *sure?*"

"What else? I heard it from a reliable source—the girl's his daughter. He got Lily in the family way, then ran off. Took shameful advantage of his brother, letting everyone think Steve had treated Annette shabbily while they were engaged."

Overcoming her shock, Fran opened her mouth, but Zach grabbed her elbow and turned her around, leading her away. The voices followed them. One belonged to Miriam Jenkins, which meant all of Tobias would know soon.

"But what will happen now? If he's the real father…"

"Ha! You think that will mean anything to someone like him? He won't want the responsibility now any more than he did eight years ago."

Fran would have gone back and confronted the women—how dare Miriam, who'd basked in his attention, who'd seen him come to Muriel's rescue—if Zach hadn't kept his hold on her.

"Well," came the other voice, "you would think a father would want to take care of his child."

"What can you expect? He ran off once, he'll do it again."

That was the last they heard. Either they had moved too far to hear the women or the women had moved to another part of the garden.

"Zach, they don't know the situation. They don't know you."

"They knew me most of my life. But it doesn't matter. What they think of me doesn't matter."

How could it not matter to him, when he had been so pleased to have these same women talking to him in the garden just a couple of weeks ago?

She took his hand, tugged him into the shed nearby, closed the door behind them, and kissed him as thoroughly and deeply as the protruding handle of a shovel and the tines of a rake would allow.

And when they agreed that they'd better get back out be-

fore they did something not only foolish but possibly dangerous in this venue, they straightened their clothes and emerged.

Walter from the country club spotted them immediately and
his eyes twinkled wickedly even as his face remained absolutely
solemn.

"Ah, Mr. Zach, that absolutely charming woman told me
I might find you here with Miss Dalton. I was hoping you
might show me the trees we discussed last week."

"Of course. But what absolutely charming woman?"

"Miss Bliss—Trudi."

Fran and Zach exchanged a lightning look of amazement,
both at the concept of Miss Trudi as absolutely charming and
at the ever-formal Walter referring to her by her first name.

Zach headed off with Walter, while Fran returned to her du-
ties in a much-improved mood. Zach was right. It truly didn't
matter what people said. But it *was* unfair.

And that injustice was the reason she snapped on Sunday.
That and the fact that the opening had been so wildly successful that they'd worked until nearly 1:00 a.m. each of the past
two nights to clean the house and restock craft items, then
were back at first light to give the grounds a quick sprucing
up before the next wave hit.

She'd told Rob flat out that Zach was going to stay with
her in her room. But they'd both been too tired to take advantage of that other than to curl up together. At least Zach
hadn't had any dreams that woke him.

So when she heard Muriel Henderson tut-tutting about
Nell being Zach's biological daughter late Sunday afternoon,
Fran was tired and perhaps feeling deprived. She marched up
to the older woman and said, "You should be ashamed of
yourself, Muriel. He took care of you when you fainted while

the rest of us stood around looking stupid. Zach has been nothing but kind to you, and besides, he's…he's a *hero*."

Everyone had left except the committee and Zach.

Fran suspected it was because none of them could move. Max and Suz sat on a bench by the back door. Annette, Steve and Miss Trudi were at one table, Rob and Kay at a second, and she and Zach at a third.

"You know," said Suz, "I kept thinking once we got to the opening that the hardest work would be over."

"A month of construction's easier than this," agreed Max.

Annette nodded. "If this keeps up, we're going to have to hire someone to run the place. Even only being open the weekends for now, how can we handle it?"

"And we'll have to be open more around the holidays," Kay said. "I was talking to this TV producer about a feature on Bliss House at Christmas…."

Everyone groaned.

"Hey, it's a great opportunity."

A loud knock interrupted her defense.

Max, the closest one to the door, heaved himself up and opened it, but not wide. He blocked the opening and said, "Sorry, you'll have to come back next weekend. We're closed."

"Oh. Too late for some publicity shots?"

"Well…" Max looked over his shoulder.

"Never too late for publicity," Kay said.

Max swung the door open, and Kay's face changed immediately.

"You!" Kay said. "Get out of here."

Fran swung around to see the tabloid reporter she'd watched retreat from her property two weeks ago advance on Zach, snapping pictures.

Zach remained where he was, his face void of expression, his eyes lifeless.

"I knew I remembered you," the man taunted. "You tried to be all high and mighty, but I remembered. There was a story—before it got taken over by the rescue of that family. But I remember faces—it's my job. And I remembered yours. What was the headline? Something like A Day with a Dead Man?"

Fran stood, trying to get between the man and Zach. "Get out." She looked to her brother. "Get him out of here."

The man continued to shoot pictures around her. And he kept talking.

"You were the one who sat with that guy who'd been crushed so bad you guys decided not to try to get him out. You were his buddy while everybody waited for him to die, right?"

Rob and Max grabbed the guy's arms, pulling him toward the door.

"How'd that feel, Zach? What was it like? Not so high and mighty now, huh?"

The two men shoved him outside and locked the door.

Steve turned to his brother, concern lining his face. "What's this about, Zach?"

Zach stood with a lurching motion, totally unlike his usual ease. "Nothing. I've gotta go."

Fran grabbed his arm. "Tell him, Zach. Tell Steve what you do, who you are."

Zach said nothing.

"He's a hero, that's who he is," Kay said.

"I'm no damned hero." Fran barely recognized Zach's hoarse voice or the dullness of his eyes. "He had it right. I sat with a man while he died. Watched him and couldn't do a damned thing except listen to his stories. Barely a day. You were with your dad for more than a year. If watching some-body die is a hero, then you're the hero, Fran."

"You know you couldn't have saved that man, Zach. You can't blame yourself. You can't."

Zach pulled free of her hold and walked out the front door.

Fran felt the hot sting of tears but didn't let them fall. She was so grateful Kay knew, because Zach wouldn't tell his story and she didn't think she could talk around the emotions tightening her throat.

"Tell them, Kay," she got out before she went after Zach. "Please, tell them."

Fran woke to the sound of heavy rain against the window. She was alone.

She hadn't been when she fell asleep. Zach had been with her then. With her, around her, in her.

She'd caught up with him outside Bliss House. Without a word, they drove home, went up the stairs and into her bedroom.

Then all he'd said was, "Fran."

It was, she was sure, a preamble to explanations that he wasn't the man she knew him to be. She stopped all the words by kissing him.

He'd engulfed her in a wave of desire and need that had her shaking inside and out. The only thing that calmed him at all was answering his passion with her own until they clung to each other as shelter within the storm they'd created.

Holding him to her, his face against her neck, her arms across his shoulders, their lower bodies still joined, she had accepted that she loved him. The final word she had held back. *Love.*

The bad-boy-gone-good, who now sat on her window seat, with one elbow on his bent knee while he stared out at the rain.

She slipped her arms into the sleeves of his shirt, closing a few strategic buttons, then went to him.

Without taking his gaze from the window, he shifted his leg, making room for her to sit facing him.

"I want her, Fran."

She brushed his hair off his forehead. "I know."

"She's my daughter, and I want to be her father. I couldn't do it the way things are now, not knowing when I might be deployed with the task force. I'd have to quit. Look for another kind of job. EMT's too irregular for a single parent alone. I could work in a hospital, maybe. Something with more regular hours. I could do that."

"You can't give up the task force, Zach. You love it."

"I'm no good anymore."

"That's crazy. That's—"

"I'd give it up. For her. I owe her."

"That isn't what you owe her, Zach."

"She's my daughter, I owe her everything."

She shook her head, repeating, "That isn't what you owe her."

"Damn it, I didn't know! If I'd known and still taken off and not been here to take care of her, or if I'd been here but let Steve take over my responsibility, then, yeah, I'd have said it was my own damn fault. But I never had a chance to be a father. Shouldn't I get a chance to be her father?"

"You're right. It's not your fault. You had no reason to think Lily was going to have your baby when you took off. And giving you the chance to be a father now would certainly be the most fair thing for you, Zach."

He looked at her for the first time, and she saw that he knew what she was going to say. Knew it, needed to hear it, and didn't want to.

"But what's the most fair thing for Nell? It's not her fault, either. All she did was be born, and form a bond with the man who's loved her from her first day of life. This is her home, Zach. This is her family."

He turned back to the window.

"I had to say it out loud once—that I could really be her father."

She touched his cheek, not sure if the track she saw there was a reflection from the window or from a tear.

"Zach, you're giving her what's most important for her to have a good and happy life. You're putting her ahead of yourself. That's what a father does."

It was a little past ten, but the rain made the night darker than usual.

Zach hung up the phone as Fran came into the kitchen.

"What is it, Zach?"

"I'm going over to talk to Steve and Annette. Nell's asleep."

"Oh."

"Will you come with me?"

"I don't think—"

"I'd like you to be there, Fran."

To be there for him.

"Yes."

It was simple, really. Much simpler than he had expected it to be.

He stood in their kitchen, just inside the door, with Fran beside him, her hand still in his from when he'd taken it as they walked under one umbrella, and he said the words.

"I wanted you both to know I won't fight for custody of

Nell. Or visitation. Not now, not ever. I'll put it in writing in whatever form you want, sign whatever papers you need."

Annette's eyes instantly filled with tears. Her mouth formed a silent *thank you*.

Steve looked at him, simply looked, but Zach saw the same emotions in his brother's eyes that were in Annette's.

Zach turned for the door, Fran's hand the only warmth in a cold, wet universe.

"Zach."

He stopped at Steve's voice, but didn't turn around.

"I have never felt as many emotions fighting each other as I did when I saw you standing in Corbett House three weeks ago. Nell's birth, marrying Annette—those were the most incredible moments of my life. But those were pure awe and joy. Seeing you…"

Zach turned now, pulled by the feeling in his brother's voice.

"I was afraid for Nell, for us—Annette and me. I was so damned angry at you for staying away. And I was more relieved than I could have thought possible."

Steve stretched his arm across the counter between them, offering his hand.

"I am so glad you've come home, Zach."

Zach put his hand in Steve's, the first time he had touched his brother in more than eight years.

Chapter Twelve

The rain was causing flooding all over the area, according to the radio announcer. Swollen streams were feeding into the Tobias River, which was expected to overflow its banks later today. But parkland bordered both sides of the river in Tobias County, and the flooding should do little damage before it emptied into the lake.

Fran wondered if the new plants at Bliss House would fare as well. She and Zach would have to go over there later and check.

Or would Zach come with her to the gardens ever again? What happened now that he'd made his decision about Nell's future? What happened to his future? What happened to them?

The network news report cut in on the radio. She didn't tune in to the announcer's voice until she heard one word.

Earthquake.

The professional voice gave the few facts known, all grim.

Heavy casualties reported, major structural damage in densely populated areas of large and poorly constructed buildings. Communication mostly cut off. But one item came through clearly—local authorities were overwhelmed.

She felt Zach behind her, sensed him listening to the radio and watching her. Chester barked outside. A light, excited bark. They ignored it.

"It's in South America. Won't they call Miami?"

"Maybe. But even if they do, our team will be on standby."

"You're going."

"Yeah."

"But you're on vacation. You told me you still have weeks of vacation time left. You told me."

"You know it's not about the job. I'm not even sure anymore…"

"Don't say that, Zach. Don't even think it. You belong on that task force."

He jerked his shoulders. "Doesn't matter now whether I do or I don't. I won't leave them shorthanded. I'm signed up for the job, and if they need me, I'll do it."

"You have to leave today?"

"Yeah."

"You're not even going to stay to say goodbye to Nell?"

"It's better this way. Not see her, just go away. I wish…" He didn't finish. "I won't ask you to wait, Fran. I don't know if I'll ever be the man to give you what you deserve."

"What about what I want?" She raised her chin. "Isn't that what you've been giving me these past days? Or was it a sex workshop after all?"

"Fran—"

"No, you listen to me, Zachary Corbett. I've been listening to you for three weeks now. Not only listening but watching and…and feeling. I know the man you are—the man you've made yourself. Yes, that's your profession, but it's more. It's who you are inside.

"That's what you've been giving me. That's what I want. That's what I deserve. No more and certainly no less. And you're the only man who can give it to me." A tiny smile curved her mouth while her eyes glittered with tears. "Bad Boy Zach Corbett with the killer baby blues, the man who steals my calm—who would have believed it?"

"Fran, I'm not the kid I was, but I'm no prince, either. When the best thing I can do for a kid is give up all rights as her father—"

A duo of barks sounded. Urgent, distressed.

Fran lifted her head. "Chester and—that sounds like Pansy."

Zach moved to the door. "It is Pansy." He craned his neck. "No sign of Nell."

Fran joined him at the door. "That's strange. Could Pansy have run off and come over here on her own?"

"Sure. But she'd also have had to open the porch door then close it behind her, because she's on the porch. I'll take her home later when I… I've got to go, Fran. I've got to get back to my job and to…figure things out. If you came to visit, or maybe I could come back here…"

Fran's clear caramel eyes gazed through him, right to his core. "It's probably better that I stay out of your way, Zach. If being around me was going to help you figure things out, it would have happened during these past weeks."

He didn't like it, but how could he argue?

The phone jerked Fran into motion. She felt stiff, awkward. She had no idea how long she'd stood in the same spot in the middle of the kitchen after Zach went upstairs to pack.

"Fran?" Annette's voice was strained. "Have you or Zach seen Nell this morning?"

"This morning? No, but Pansy's here on my porch."

"Pansy…? Oh. I… Oh, Fran."

"Annette? What's wrong?"

"The school called. Nell's not there."

Fran looked at the clock. It was almost an hour after Nell should have arrived at school.

"Maybe she's at Corbett House."

"I'll call there next. But…this is so unlike her. And the rain—oh, Fran…"

"You call Corbett House and Steve. I'll be right there. And Zach. We'll be right there."

Before she had the receiver in place, she was already shouting, "Zach! Zach!"

The rain didn't so much fall as drop on them, as if they stood beneath a drainpipe as large as the sky. Just the dash from the back porch to Steve and Annette's house soaked them.

Fran and Zach ducked inside the open garage door and into the kitchen from there. Annette acknowledged them with the smallest nod and continued talking on the phone.

"No, Steve. No one has seen her…. The school, Fran and Zach, Miss Trudi, your mother…. Yes…. Yes, as soon as you can— No, wait, Steve. Someone should talk to her friend, Laura Ellen. Laura Ellen's in school, but if this is something Nell's been thinking about… Yes, I'll stay here. Call me if you… Yes, yes. You, too. And, Steve—drive carefully."

Her hands shook as she replaced the receiver. She pressed them against the edge of the counter. "Thank you for coming."

"Of course we came." Fran placed her hand on top of Annette's. "We'll do whatever we can."

Zach turned from the calendar boards posted on the wall. "Was there something today she didn't want to do, that would've made her skip school? Could she have gotten confused—gone to some event the wrong day?"

Annette shook her head throughout the questions. "We talked about what she was doing today—she knew what she was doing and was looking forward to it."

He grunted acceptance. "Use your cell phone from now on, in case she calls."

"Of course, you're right."

"Have you called the police?"

"No. Do you think—?"

"Call them. What was she wearing?"

"Jeans and a light blue top. A dark green slicker with a hood, her black backpack. Oh, and yellow rain boots."

"Good. What's her path to school?"

She told him, but added, "I drove it twice after the school called. There's something else—she was going to walk to school, but her bike's gone."

"Is Steve stopping to talk to her friend on his way home?"

She nodded. "I'm going to call Laura Ellen's mother, too."

"Good idea. But call the police first—don't worry about it being a false alarm, we'll apologize later." Zach wiped the board marked Next Month clean, grabbed a blue marker and made a rough outline of Lake Tobias and the town. With the red marker he added crossed dotted lines, creating quadrants. "I'm starting here." He added a red *Z* in the area they were in. "Any volunteers who want to look, you put them in a new quadrant. Once you have people in each quadrant, start halving them. If you have more than eight volunteers, start halving the halves. Understand?"

"Yes, but…"

"Zach works in search and rescue, Annette," Fran said. "He knows what to do."

Zach checked his cell phone's battery. He grabbed a note-pad and wrote his name and cell number. "Keep a roster of everybody's phone numbers. Start a list on another sheet of everything you've done and everyone you've talked to, plus what they said."

He looked at Fran for the first time. Pain pressed at her throat. His eyes looked as if the blue had shattered, leaving only glints amid a murky dullness.

"Stay here with Annette, Fran. Call if you hear anything."

He walked out without another word. For half a second, Fran remained still. Then she squeezed Annette's hands and said, "I'll be right back."

"Zach!"

He was halfway down the driveway, but turned back to her. Kay's car pulled up to the curb, and Fran saw Miss Trudi in the passenger seat.

"Zach, the thing with Pansy being on the porch... If Nell was on the porch, if she left Pansy, she might have heard you say you were leaving."

"I know." His voice was raw. "Tell Annette and Steve about it, and the police when they come. I should've... I've gotta go look for her, Fran."

He spun away.

He was blaming himself. And she could do nothing to help him.

Rain dripped from her hair and down her cheeks like tears as she watched Zach back his car out of her driveway and pull away.

Rescues didn't happen because you wanted them to. They happened because you knew your job, did your work and cooperated with everyone around you. And because you had some damned good luck.

So, crawling up one street and down another, methodical and focused, Zach prayed.

He prayed he wouldn't need his skills. He prayed his skills would be up to whatever was needed. He prayed for damned good luck.

He prayed this would be different.

He hadn't saved Elliott. He hadn't saved Miguel. Please, God, let him save Nell.

His cell phone rang. His heart jammed against his ribs in hope and fear.

"Corbett here."

"Zach." It was Steve, and Zach knew immediately it was neither the worst nor the best of news. "Fran said to give you a message."

Fran's clear eyes had gazed right through him, right to his core. *If being around me was going to help you figure things out, it would have happened during these past weeks.*

"Fran's not there?"

Rain hit the windshield like fingernails tapping to get in.

"No. She left half an hour ago. We've been trying to get you, but couldn't get a signal to your phone. She said to tell you she was going to look for Nell over where we used to go for raspberries. I told her Nell's never been there, so I don't know why. But Fran insisted and said to call you."

"Okay. Thanks. No other word?"

"No. Just a lot of… We've eliminated a lot of places. The police are looking, too."

"Good. We'll find her, Steve. We'll find your daughter."

He clicked off; there wasn't anything else to say. He turned the car around and headed for the old bridge over the Tobias

River, where he and Rob and Steve had gone picking raspberries as kids.

Steve didn't know why Nell might go there, but Zach did.

Because he'd told her about the place where he and Steve had been the best of brothers.

He followed the path they used to take as kids, bouncing over clumps of vegetation and mounds of earth until the car wouldn't fit between the tree trunks.

Wishing to hell he had even half the equipment he kept in his car at home, he tucked what he did have into the pockets of his jacket. The flashlight, first-aid kit, bottled water, Swiss Army knife and expandable insulated blanket were among the supplies he'd bought from the discount store and stashed in the car when he'd first arrived in Tobias. He pulled on an extra pair of gardening gloves.

He needed them immediately. The wild raspberry bushes were bare to their arching, iridescent purple canes. They grabbed at him, clinging even more than the ones at Bliss House. These canes were lithe, twisting back to catch him in a new place whenever he freed himself.

He pushed through, letting them rip.

Don't be so impatient, Zach.

It was Steve's voice. A boy's voice.

A flash of heat enveloped him. It was summer. The smell of sun-warmed raspberries, the sting of pricks into his sweat-encrusted skin. Steve was reaching carefully into the thicket, plucking berries one by one until he had a handful, then drawing his hand out.

Next time don't go plunging in and you won't get stuck so bad. Take your time.

Not now. There wasn't time to take. He had to find Nell. And Fran. Plunging in was the only way.

Yellow. He could swear he saw a flash of yellow.

Pushing and crashing through wet canes, he clambered to a slick spit of bank beside the river. The rush of water chewed away at the shoreline with the frenzied bites of a starved man handed a steak.

And there, on a small island that extended from the central stone upright of the old bridge, stood Nell and Fran. Fran was bent over, protecting Nell from the rain with her body. Water gushed around either side of the upright, making constant inroads on the island.

"Fran!"

She lifted her head, but didn't see him.

"Fran! Over here."

She spotted him, waved acknowledgement. Through the slanting rain he now saw the pale oval of Nell's face under the hood of her slicker.

Fran shouted something. It sounded like "We're okay."

"I'm coming to get you!"

Even as he shouted the promise, he punched in 9-1-1 on his cell phone. He told the dispatcher the situation and the location.

"We'll send someone right away," she said. "Stay on the line with me. Don't try to do anything until the experts arrive."

He hung up. He was the expert. And there wasn't time to wait for equipment.

On this side of the river the embankment beside the old road had eroded away to a sheer drop. He'd have to backtrack and circle wide to get to a point where he could climb up to the road. And even then, he'd be above them, with no way to reach them.

He had to go across.

He went as far upriver as the bank would take him, but he'd still be swimming at an angle against the current.

Closer now, he could see Fran and Nell more clearly. Fran shouted something, but he couldn't hear because the sound of the water pounding the bridge supports made too much noise.

He stripped off his jacket, put his supplies in it and tied it into as tight a bundle as he could, then threaded his belt through it and put the belt back around his waist.

He tightened the knots in his shoelaces—he needed the shoes to protect him from debris tumbling through the river — then looked once more at Fran and Nell on the small island, and plunged in.

Cold, roaring water slammed into him. He swam in short, choppy strokes, his arms close to his head, but still the flotsam battered him.

His lungs burned, his arms felt weighted, but he pushed through the rushing water, stumbling onto the island, to Fran's steadying hands.

"Any injuries?" He got out the question between gulps of air.

"No. We're okay." Fran helped him unhook the bundle and gave Nell a drink of water, then him. "She was trying to cross the river—to the raspberries."

He nodded. The "whys" could wait.

"We're going to get you guys off this island paradise."

"That sounds like a good idea." Thank God for Fran's calm.

He looked up, judging the distance to the bridge's concrete railing overhead.

"It's too high," Fran said into his ear. "I tried boosting her to my shoulders, but it was way too far."

He nodded. "Help's coming, but we're not waiting. I'll swim Nell across, and you—"

"I'm not a good swimmer, Zach. I…I wouldn't make…"

"Okay. I'll come back for you then."

"Zach, you're exhausted...."

Their eyes met, and he saw her recognize the fact that there was no other way. There was barely room for the three of them to stand on this fast-disappearing island, and once it went, there would be nothing to hold on to.

"I'll take the shorter route this time," he said with a flicker of a grin. He crouched to the girl's level.

"Okay, Nell. I'm going to swim you across the river. You're going to hold on to me tight, and stay as close as possible. Understand?"

She glared at him.

He saw the fear in her expression, the awareness of danger. But she didn't panic, this girl he'd helped create. And she was ticked.

"You don't want me. I heard you. You're going away because you don't want me."

"No—"

"I heard you! I heard you. You're going away. You said so."

"Nell—that's not because of you. Do you hear me? I don't live here anymore. I live somewhere else. That's where my job is—that's why I'm going away."

"But..." Her chin wobbled and tears tracked down through the rain on her cheeks. "You and Daddy are mad at each other. You aren't like real brothers, like when you used to come here. And it's 'cause of me."

"It can take grown-ups longer to get over things than kids. It's going to take us a while to be okay. But when we do, I think we'll be better brothers than before. Now listen to me." He brought his face close to hers, looking into a reflection of his own eyes. "I know this has been confusing for you. But you're a smart kid, and you know the right way for all this to sort out. Your daddy's your true father. And your mommy is Annette. You're a family. If you didn't have them, I would never let you go, never in this lifetime. But you do."

"Wh-what about you?"

"Me? I'm your uncle. Your Uncle Zach, who loves you, too. Always will." He straightened. "And now we're going to swim, and you're going to do everything I tell you. Understand?"

She nodded, tears still in her eyes, but the chin solid once more.

He left the bundle with Fran, wrapping her in the insulated blanket and kissing her once before she helped him hook his belt through the loops of Nell's jeans to hold her close to his downriver side. He'd use his body to protect her from the debris. He instructed Nell to float, to hold on tight and not to fight him. She stepped out of the yellow boots he'd first spotted and they waded in.

She gasped when the water struck her. When he glanced down, though, she had her lip between her teeth and not another sound came out.

He wished to hell he was the swimmer Steve was.

It was shorter to this bank, but the trip was harder. He was tired. He was trying to protect Nell, and he was basically swimming for two, though he felt her kicking her legs beside him.

Halfway across, something whacked his arm and he faltered, dipping Nell's face under the water. She came up sputtering, but her legs never quit kicking.

"Okay?"

"Okay."

Neither had breath for more than that.

He felt ground under his feet at last, but the river had risen over the grassy bank so it was slippery as ice. He clambered up using one hand, while the other arm encircled Nell's slight form and pushed her higher above the water. At last they scrambled to solid ground, both gulping in air.

He allowed himself ten deep breaths, then unhooked the belt with hands that weren't functioning properly. He felt as if his fingers had swollen to four times their size. Finally, Nell was free.

"Nell, you get up to the old road, and you wait there. Help is coming."

"But—"

"Do what you're told."

"Okay...Uncle Zach."

"Good." He gave her a boost and watched for two seconds as she pulled herself up the steep incline, gripping the sturdy saplings and bushes. She was a tough kid, his...niece.

He turned around and started back into the water. This time he heard Fran's clear shout of "No!"

The debris was so thick now he could barely find water to stroke through. Branches slapped at him, leaves plastered his face.

There'd be no crossing this river another time. Fran would be pummeled.

A log slammed into him, swinging his arm out of the way like it was nothing, then scraped across the back of his head and rolled down his body. He went under. All the way under.

He heard a voice. Elliott. *You've done good work, boy.* Yes, it was Elliott. Zach saw his face. The sun-weathered wrinkles, the pallor of illness, and those eyes that gave no quarter. Then another face. Miguel. Pain twisting his features, words flowing from him as peace seemed to flow into him.

But then Zach saw other faces. A few faces he'd helped pull from rubble that would have been a grave otherwise. But mostly faces far more familiar. Guys on the task force. Doc,

Taz and Waco. Rob and Kay. Max and Suz. Miss Trudi. His mother. Steve and Annette. Nell. And Fran…Fran.

He stroked through the water, pulling, reaching up. Again and again. He surfaced, gulping in air, taking in water with it, coughing, pulling in more air.

And he kept stroking, reaching. He didn't even know where he was heading anymore. He had to keep going.

He felt something at his shoulder. More debris?

"Oh, God, Zach. Zach!"

It was Fran.

Hands pulled at him. He dug his feet in and staggered upright, held half by her, half by the bridge support.

"Zach, you should have stayed there. Why did you do this?"

His chest heaved with the effort to form words. "Because you're here."

She gasped. He thought it might have been a sob. "That log… I thought— I thought—oh, God, Zach."

She wrapped her arms around him and they held each other. He wanted to stay there forever, or for at least the half of forever it would take for his lungs and muscles to recover.

But he felt the water lapping over his shoes and knew there was no time left.

"Climb up on my shoulders, Fran. The two of us might be tall enough for you to reach the railing."

"No. I'm not leaving you. I'm—"

He held her face between his hands. "Fran. We need to try. We need help."

She looked up, then back at him. They had to try.

Tears welled in her eyes as she nodded.

He bent over, bracing his hands against the support so he'd have help straightening if he needed it. Fran crouched beside him, turning his face to her. Their bodies created a small pocket of quiet.

"You should know that I love you, Zach Corbett."

He tried to say the words, but they wouldn't come. He kissed her, their lips cold and wet, and he never wanted to stop.

And then she straightened, patted his back, and swung her leg up.

"Stand up!" he shouted.

He felt her wobbling, but she stood, steadying herself against the rough surface of the bridge.

He pressed his feet into the soggy ground, straightening his legs, slow, steady. If he jerked or slipped—but he wouldn't. He would do what he needed to save Fran. Fran had to be safe. Had to.

In increments that took seconds but seemed to last lifetimes, he brought himself upright, feeling Fran's shifting balance on his shoulders. She called out—words he couldn't decipher, though she sounded excited. But her weight didn't shift the way it would if she were reaching for the railing.

And then it not only shifted, but lifted off, so abruptly that he stumbled sideways. His foot went out from under him and he dropped to his knees, one in the water, one on the last patch of the island.

"Zach!"

It was a chorus of his name. He looked up, and saw faces looking down at him over the railing. A dozen voices calling his name. A rope came over the side, snaking down to him.

He pulled himself up, made a loop in the end and fit it under his arms. He tightened the knot, grabbed hold of the rope above him, and shouted "Ready!"

He felt the slow draw on the rope. His feet cleared the water, which now covered the ground they'd stood on. He dangled, cold water streaming from his shoes, then was slowly pulled upward.

As Zach neared the railing, he saw Fran's face, pale, intense. He tried to grin at her, but he didn't think his mouth cooperated.

Steve, straddling the railing, leaned over and grabbed his arm, hauling him up so other hands could secure him and bring him onto the cracked surface of the old bridge.

"Nell?"

"She's fine," Steve said. "She's in a car with Annette and the heater's going full blast."

He nodded—at least he thought he did. Fran was beside him. He took her hand.

The buzz of voices and bustle of activity seemed to push away from him then. Like a radio turned low.

They made him sit down, but he kept hold of Fran's hand, so she sat with him. Someone put a blanket around him; she tucked it tighter. She was cocooned in a blanket, too. Someone else gave him a cup with hot coffee. He scalded his tongue on the sugary substance, and didn't care.

"Let me take a look at that head," instructed a woman in a uniform.

"Bleeding?" he asked.

"Sure is," she said cheerfully. "Along with a bunch of bark stuck to it."

He winced once at the sting of the antiseptic she applied. "It's okay," he reassured Fran.

"You could use stitches," the paramedic said. "But it'll do for now."

A small form came barreling toward him. Zach stood to meet her, still holding Fran's hand, glad for Steve's support.

"Okay, Steve?" He met his brother's eyes. Knew his question was understood.

"Yeah. Okay."

Nell wrapped her arms around Zach, burying her face against him so he had no chance of understanding what she said. But he heard his name a couple times, and what sounded like "Uncle." He stroked her wet hair and patted her on the back. They were going to be okay.

Another figure hurried through the pockets of official and unofficial rescuers.

Water streamed her hair flat, formed dark stains on her designer suit.

"Nell! Zach! Oh, thank God, thank God!"

Lana Corbett hurled herself at him. He had to let go of Fran's hand to hold on to his mother.

"They said Nell was in the river, they said it was rising… Thank you. For saving our girl."

He took the blanket off his shoulders, turned it inside out and put it around Lana, his hands lingering.

And then Lana Corbett reached out and put her palm against her younger son's cheek, and he was sure those were tears. She looked up, up to heavens still streaming rain. "Thank you for bringing all my family back safely."

"Fran." They were in the back of Steve's SUV with fresh, dry blankets wrapped around them.

"Yes, Zach."

"I won't lose you again."

"You didn't lose me this time."

She cupped her hand to the hard line of his jaw, grazing her thumb across his top lip.

His head came up, their eyes met. She tipped her head, her fingers so light against his jaw, and kissed him. After too brief a time, she lifted her head and looked at him again.

"We're getting married."

She grinned. "Is that an order?"

He wasn't ready to grin yet. "Damn right it's an order. We're getting married."

"Okay, but it has to be in Bliss House, or Miss Trudi will never forgive us."

"I don't care where. If you don't want to leave here, Fran—"

"I want to go where there are plenty of universities and white picket fences and you. I hear Virginia's the place for all that."

This time, she put her hands on his shoulders and kissed him completely. Exploring angles and connections, lining his bottom lip, then meeting his tongue. His arms came around her.

"It's not an easy life, Fran. There's a lot of time spent away from the family. The ones staying at home carry the whole load, and we never know when we might be called or—"

"You don't think I can handle it?"

"I know you can handle anything. I just want to let you know what it is you'll have to be handling."

"I can handle you, Zach Corbett, and that's what matters."

Oh, yeah, she most definitely could handle him.

* * * * *

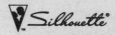

SPECIAL EDITION™

is proud to present a dynamic new voice in romance, Jessica Bird, with the first of her Moorehouse family trilogy.

BEAUTY AND THE BLACK SHEEP

Available July 2005

The force of those eyes hit Frankie Moorehouse like a gust of wind. But she quickly reminded herself that she had dinner to get ready, a staff (such as it was) to motivate, a busines to run. She didn't have the luxury of staring into a stranger's face.

Although, jeez, what a face it was.

And wasn't it just her luck that *he* was the chef her restaurant desperately needed, and he was staying the summer....

Where love comes alive™

If you enjoyed what you just read,
then we've got an offer you can't resist!

Take 2 bestselling love stories FREE!

Plus get a FREE surprise gift!

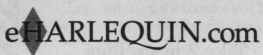